THE LADY IN THE CASTLE

R.L. Tecklenburg

THE LADY IN THE
CASTLE

HISTRIA
FICTION

Histria Fiction

Las Vegas ◊ London ◊ New York ◊ Palm Beach

Published in the United States of America by
Histria Books
7181 N. Hualapai Way, Ste. 130-86
Las Vegas, NV 89166 USA
HistriaBooks.com

Histria Fiction is an imprint of Histria Books. Titles published under the imprints of Histria Books are distributed in the United States and Canada by Simon & Schuster and worldwide through Unified Book Distribution. We appreciate your support of copyright by purchasing an authorized edition of this book and for respecting intellectual property laws by not reproducing, scanning, or otherwise distributing any part of it by any means without permission. You are supporting authors and enabling Histria Books to continue publishing books for everyone.

All rights reserved. No part of this book may be reprinted or reproduced or utilized in any form or by any electronic, mechanical or other means, now known or hereafter invented, including photocopying and recording, or in any information storage or retrieval system, without the permission in writing from the Publisher. No part of this book may be used or reproduced in any manner for the purpose of training artificial intelligence technologies or systems.

Certain characters in this work are historical figures, and certain events portrayed did take place. However, this is a work of fiction. Names, characters, places, and incidents are either the product of the author's imagination or are used fictitiously. Any resemblance to actual persons, living or dead, is entirely coincidental.

First Edition

Library of Congress Control Number: 2023938041

ISBN 978-1-59211-680-5 (softbound)
ISBN 978-1-59211-339-2 (eBook)

Copyright © 2026 by R.L. Tecklenburg

For Rebecca

Schloss Itter

...In that will be a legacy Worthy of our sacrifice And a monument

Fit to mark

The end of our war...

— Steve Mason, "A History Lesson," from *Johnny's Song*, 1986, p. 53

PREFACE

It is with pride and great sorrow that I tell you the story of Castle Itter, and of the men and woman—soldiers and civilians, French, American, Austrian, and Czech—who fought so heroically against a German Panzer battalion. Behind those medieval stone walls, we gave our all to wage the final European battle of World War II.

We—each of us who survived—in our own way went on to live our lives, but we struggled with memories of that day. For me, it was the pain of losing my husband along with others defending the castle in a battle that was not only the last of the war, but perhaps the most unnecessary.

Castle Itter jealously guards the memories of more than 700 years of history. Knights, counts, servants, soldiers, and prisoners—defenders and attackers—have fought, bled, and died on these grounds, and like ghosts, walk the castle halls, stone stairways, and the many rooms shrouded in darkness.

Like the others, I, too, am trapped in its history. Yet, I know I will never be alone.

Maria Von Eickler May 5, 2000

CHAPTER 1

March 10, 1945

The thin yet beautiful young woman slowly dragged herself along with the others in a line three abreast that stretched a city block. Shuffling along with Austrians, Hungarians, and Slovakians, all with few pieces of clothing and triangle-shaped badges pinned to their chests, she thought about Josef and wondered if he was alive or killed. The last she heard from him, his unit was in southern France, fighting the American and British armies. Paris fell to the enemy, and the Wehrmacht retreated across the whole of France for the Belgium border and Rhine River. That was almost seven months ago. He is dead. I feel it in my heart, Maria thought, as the line inched toward the railroad tracks.

"Hey you, traitor!" a soldier yelled at her. "Keep alert." He nudged her with his Mauser.

Soldiers stood in front of the line. They yelled and pointed. "Men in one line and women to another," they barked. A light flurry of snow fell gently on the cobblestone street touching everyone—captor and prisoner.

The ancient wood platform of the rail station suddenly shuddered as a steam locomotive and ten boxcars arrived from the east. The screech of a long, high-pitched whistle quickly got everyone's attention. Maria saw the red boxcars lining the tracks. Workers in gray uniforms ran to throw open the long side doors.

The long lines of prisoners reached the trains and halted, waiting meekly for the guards to give further orders. Maria saw an old red railcar immediately in front of her, the long side door open. Inside, there was only darkness.

"Come on, come on, move it," an SS guard in his black uniform yelled, speaking a dialect of German with which she was not familiar. She witnessed him push an old woman ahead of her.

"Leave her," Maria called to the guard. "Can't you see she is very elderly?" The woman could not navigate the steep steps into the boxcar. She wore a yellow star pinned to her breast. Recognizing its meaning, Maria knew she was a Jew. Her badge was red, which signified a political prisoner. Looking around most wore the yellow badge, but she also noticed a few green and a pink star on one young man. She did not know its meaning but could easily guess.

"Help her, traitor," the guard ordered Maria. "And hurry. You're holding up the line." He pulled a watch from his pocket and read the time. Maria quickly stepped forward to help the woman. Both entered the interior darkness, and the car began quickly to fill.

Outside in front of a connecting car, the guard's shepherd dog began to bark. It growled threateningly at an old man also trying to get into a car. The dog growled until his handler stepped forward to survey the situation.

"Old man, get in now or I will shoot you where you stand." A prisoner behind him, much younger, stepped forward to assist.

The day began shadowy and very damp. A light snow continued to fall and had been falling since the early dawn hours when they dragged her from her cell. Maria shivered in the frosty air. She was dressed only in a coarse woven shift and someone else's shoes the guards had given her, but no coat or hat.

Now, as the boxcar filled with people, the temperature rose quickly. The odor of unbathed bodies dressed in soiled clothing most disturbed her as they squeezed together tighter and tighter in the confined space. She had never experienced anything like it before. *I guess my life has been very sheltered and protected. I could not accept the rumors,* she thought, stunned by the utter brutality around her.

The Fascists had arrested her only days earlier protecting an American pilot in their large country home. A servant in her father-in-law's home had betrayed her to the local Home Guard. They subjected her to a brutality and indecency she never dreamed she would have to experience.

She had never accepted Hitler or his wars. She saw her husband, Josef, conscripted into the Wehrmacht, and his stepbrother, Kurt, marched off to join the Waffen SS. She and his father, Rolf, found it difficult to forgive Kurt for becoming a card-carrying Nazi, but they quietly and cooperatively went along with the Fascist program. Then, in fall of '44, everything changed. The disruptions, bombings, and loss of lives—of both civilians and soldiers—became unbearable.

Maria had enough and decided she must act. She and her father-in-law became more involved in local resistance activities. She gave partisans operating in the area aid and comfort that included food and shelter, but on several occasions, she acted as courier, smuggling messages to the Allies, a small cog in a long chain to pass vital information.

Trusted servants notified her immediately when the American fighter plane crashed in a meadow near Rolf's great estate. Antiaircraft fire from the German positions around Vienna struck the plane a few kilometers away from Krems, a village near the estate. Both the pilot and copilot bailed out. Maria found one man already dead. His chute had failed to open, Rolf told her. The other man landed safely, but as they soon discovered, suffered a broken leg as well as multiple rib fractures. With Rolf agreeing, Maria decided quickly to rescue and protect him until he was healthy enough to find his way to Switzerland. They knew well the risk they were taking. Before they could get the pilot to safety, four men dressed as civilians whom she did not recognize, came to their door and arrested her. She endured a week in the filthy town jail. A disgruntled servant had betrayed her.

The Gestapo soon arrived—mousy-looking men in dark trench coats. Their interrogation began immediately and was relentless and brutal. Maria could not believe they were even human. They asked the same questions repeatedly until they got the answers they desired. Mostly, they asked about American and Russian contacts in the area. Who was the local leader of the partisan group? They beat her, stripped her, and then raped her when they were satisfied they had what they wanted. On and on it went. Home Guard members, many of whom she grew up with, stood by and said nothing while the Gestapo brutalized her.

Telling her she had betrayed her husband off fighting on the Western Front; Guard members shaved her head and paraded her down the streets of their small village near Krems, Austria. Boys, only boys, she thought. All eligible males were drafted into the Wehrmacht.

They wanted to humiliate her and force her into confinement until the war ended, but not kill her. Everyone knew the horrible war would end sooner rather than later.

The Gestapo ordered that she be shot immediately, but the Home Guard refused to allow that in the village, knowing that Rolf, the wealthiest landowner in the vicinity, would object vehemently.

Maria learned after seven years living in Hitler's Third Reich that the Nazi sympathizers in the village spied and would betray anyone, especially the Jews, but they could never look someone in the eyes and then shoot them. That kind of action took a special person. They were called the SS, and the Gestapo was the worst. The Home Guard's actions witnessed every day were cowardly and stupid, driven by fear and jealousy. But the Gestapo was pure evil, driven by anger and hate. They hated the Jews, and they despised anyone who threatened the Reich and their position in it. They ruled Austria under Himmler by 1945.

She warned Rolf repeatedly of their danger. She recognized too late that she should have paid more attention to her own warnings.

The townspeople knew her father-in-law would punish them severely for their actions so everyone—"undesirables" and political prisoners—were turned over to the Gestapo. The Gestapo captain, with the Commander of the Home Guard unit acquiescing, decided to ship her to Dachau for the execution. She would simply disappear like thousands of others under the Nazi Regime. Dachau, the concentration camp where the

Nazis shipped political prisoners, was only several hours away by train. With the Russians in Poland, they now shipped everyone there.

She heard coughing which worsened as the guards forced more and more captives into the narrow confines of the dirty car. She heard no weeping or praying. That surprised her at first, then she decided the others had accepted their fate much like her. And, like the others, she knew what awaited her. We are dead and this we cannot escape, she told herself. We have gone beyond fear, and now I must accept my sentence. Maria had always known the punishment for her betrayal of Hitler if they caught her.

Quickly the boxcars filled and could hold no more bodies. The side door slammed shut and locked, casting everyone in complete darkness. Minutes later, the car jerked as the locomotive built up steam to move forward. Quiet reigned, but soon, Maria heard whispers and cries from children. The coughing resumed.

The elderly woman Maria assisted into the car nudged her. It seemed to Maria she wanted to speak, so she bent down to hear.

"Why? You are not a Jew," she asked, tapping Maria's red badge.

Maria did not know how to respond. She had to consider. "The Gestapo sent me."

The old woman nodded, appearing to understand. "I think we are both beyond the reach of even God. He has forsaken us, and now we are alone without hope."

The heat and the odor of dozens of human beings packed together became stifling as the train, filled beyond capacity with its doomed passengers, chugged onward toward Dachau, its final destination.

"You are a political prisoner," the old woman said. "It must have taken great courage to defy Hitler. You will die a hero. You must hold onto that."

Maria looked hard at the woman. "Still, I will die."

"I have lived long," the woman said. "And I've seen much. I am the last in my family. They took the others—my husband, children—from me. I have had time to think about death, and I know some ways are far worse than others." She raised her head to look at Maria, saw her crudely shorn locks, the simple soiled shift, and finally the sadness in her eyes. "What is your name, girl?"

"Maria Von Eickler, but my name is no longer of importance. I will die nameless without even a stone in an ancient cemetery to remind others that I have lived."

The old woman straightened and grabbed Maria's wrist with her trembling hand. "You have freely chosen how to live your life and did so with honor. That is why the Fascists must kill you. They can shoot you, but they cannot ever destroy your spirit unless you allow them. Maria Von Eickler is only a name, a tag. It does not say that you are an honorable and heroic woman for fighting them. We must resist them for as long as we can. The war will end soon. Believe that."

"I wish the SS could understand that and stop it now," Maria replied. They did not speak again.

Having parked herself near the door along the wooden side where the air seemed lighter, Maria kneeled slightly and closed her eyes. She thought about Josef and Kurt, when they were younger. The world seemed lighter; a spark of hope still hung in the air. That was before March 1938, the Anschluss, when Hitler marched his troops into Austria, and the Nazi leader, Arthur Seyss-Inquart declared himself head of the government. They spent that summer high in the woods near the Czech border in a small cottage Kurt's father, Rolf, owned. A final holiday before the storm.

She sadly smiled as memories flooded back. She closed her eyes to enjoy them, a brief escape from the horrors surrounding her. She swam in a small pond on the property naked, with Josef at her side. That was something she had never done. That summer Josef told her he loved her. They vowed to run off to Paris and become Bohemians before Hitler could catch them. Then the war came.

Kurt, an ardent nationalist had joined the Nazi Party. They assigned him political tasks immediately. He prepared for the new regime and knew he had an important role, as a defender of the Third Reich. In 1940, Josef was drafted to fight for Hitler. They were married only a few days before he shipped out with his unit. Maria stayed behind to care for Rolf and run the estate. Their world had changed forever.

It was almost five years since they were married, but they had been together as man and wife only several weeks. Now he is probably dead, buried in an unmarked grave somewhere in France, she feared.

She felt a hand on her shoulder. Maria's eyes sprang open. Startled, she jumped back reflexively. "Who?" she asked, seeing a younger woman pinned with the yellow star standing directly in front of her. "What do you want?"

"Only conversation. You do not recognize me?" the young woman replied.

Maria tried to see the young woman's features in the darkness. "You… your father is the tailor… Simon. Why?"

"We are Jews."

"Your family?" Maria asked.

"My husband and son are in another car. I don't know if I'll ever see them again. My father was shot last year. My mother?" She shrugged. "I don't know… Auschwitz probably."

"I'm sorry."

"I have news for you. Bad news."

"What can be worse? But tell me, what is it?"

"I saw you in the street after they captured you. I was surprised. Then I heard… my husband heard about your father-in-law."

"What?" Maria believed he was safe.

"Three days ago, he died of a heart attack. They say the Gestapo came for him.

He fought them, died fighting them. I'm sorry for your loss."

Maria's heart sank. She slumped back against the wood. Tears flowed freely. *But what does it matter now?* She forced herself to act stoically, staring at nothing. *The war..., so close to its end. They fear the Russians and must hide their terrible crimes. They must take everyone west,* she thought looking around at the mass of humans crowded together.

"This is a train filled with walking dead," Maria said. "We can only pray our lives had some meaning. That is all we have left," she said to anyone who cared to listen.

CHAPTER 2

They again heard the screech of the steam whistle as the train slowed. Everyone seemed to know they had reached their final destination—Dachau. Fear was etched deep on everyone's face, Maria knew. The whispering and even the children's cries stopped.

The wheels on the steam engine reversed and the train slowly stopped with a jerk and thud.

Within seconds, the old wooden doors slid open, and soldiers began to yell again.

"Get out! Get out now! If you cannot, we will shoot you where you stand!" a younger, baby-faced SS guard yelled. The car emptied quickly, leaving only the disabled and very old behind.

Maria looked for the old woman in the line forming up. She did not see her.

She has chosen her death, Maria thought sadly.

"In line! Everyone in line. Women here and men over there." Two SS guards stood between two lines of women as they stepped from the cars. Two more guards watched as men vacated their car.

Rows of single-story buildings neatly organized emerged in the dense fog surrounded by high fences of barbed wire. Towers dominated the perimeter. For Maria, the place reeked of suffering and death.

The train of prisoners had arrived at Dachau, 16 kilometers northwest of Munich, operated by the Schutzstaffel (SS). Two SS soldiers in their black uniforms stood in the shadows and watched the prisoners disembark. A captain and the camp commander observed as a lower ranking soldier selected women from the line forming and moving slowly into the light provided by towering spotlights.

The captain, using a cane for support, thought he recognized a face—a beautiful face although bruised with blond hair crudely cut short. He walked nearer the line for a closer look at the young woman, but he said nothing to her. The woman looked at the gravel as she shuffled forward. She did not see the SS officer looking at her. The captain saw the red piece of cloth pinned to her frock that exclaimed "Verräter." He frowned.

Both the guard and the camp commander continued to watch. The guard stepped forward. "Careful Captain," he said. "Disease is everywhere among them. Typhus."

The captain nodded. "Colonel, that one." He pointed to Maria. "She looks healthy. I think she will do nicely."

The guard grabbed her by the arm and jerked her from the line. "What is her name?" the captain asked.

The guard looked at the officer, curious that he should want to know, then shrugged. "Speak woman! What is your name?"

Maria, still looking down without making any eye contact, said, "My name? I have none. For the dead it does not matter."

The guard pushed her, and Maria fell back against another prisoner.

"No, please…" the woman, older than Maria, said, frightened. She looked behind her for support but received none from the woman behind her. The woman wore the yellow star and carried a bundle that they did not take from her. She appeared to be alone.

"Keep moving there," another guard ordered.

The guard smiled. "Yes, you're right. You need no name anymore, do you, traitor and spy for the Bolsheviks. They should have shot you already. Now you waste our time."

SS Captain Kurt Schrader and the camp commandant, SS Colonel Wilhelm Waldheim still watched the prisoners file past, but Captain Schrader kept a close eye on Maria.

The prisoners stopped abruptly. A woman in front had fallen. A guard dragged her from the line, kicking her mercilessly.

The two officers saw that the prisoners were sickly and starved. With food scarce throughout the Reich and disease rampant, each shipment became worse than those arriving earlier, especially from the East. Both knew the train would be one of the last as the Allies closed in from both directions. "Typhus will do your job for you, Herr Colonel," Schrader commented. He was careful to stand more than several feet away from the prisoners. He knew the disease was a killer. He had seen it during his service on the Eastern Front.

"Good, good, we have few men left to guard them and bullets are scarce." "Commandant Wimmer needs three replacements. He desires one woman and two men, Herr Colonel," Captain Schrader said. "He will use the woman as a personal servant for our French guests, and the two men for maintenance around the castle. I will personally transport them to Schloss Itter."

"What has happened to the others I sent only a few weeks ago, Captain?" "Two were shot trying to escape, and the other was returned."

"Too much freedom for these degenerates, eh Captain?" Colonel Waldheim replied sarcastically.

"Yes, yes, of course," Captain Schrader said, seeing no humor in the colonel's words. "The woman, sir?"

"Take her. What do I care?"

"Sergeant, bring the woman here," Captain Schrader ordered.

The sergeant reached over and grabbed the woman. He pulled her from the line to drag her over to the two officers.

"Let go of me. I demand that you leave me alone, swine." She fought against his grip, but resistance was useless, and the guard easily overpowered her.

He deposited her in front of the officers. "Herr Captain, is this the woman you want? See the tag? She is a traitor to the Fatherland and under orders to be shot. You cannot… "

"Yes, yes, Sergeant. Leave her."

The sergeant saluted, turned, and walked away. *She'll get what she deserves, and I don't have to bother with a firing squad. Makes my life easier,* he thought.

For the first time, Maria looked up and recognized the younger man in front of her. She did not speak. She stared at Schrader, as if she was hallucinating.

Captain Schrader looked her over. He saw that she was dressed poorly, without a coat in the frigid Bavarian winter. He saw bruises on her face and arms. The Gestapo had sheared her blond hair. "A shame. Her beautiful long hair," Schrader said softly.

"Do you speak French," he asked her, but knew well she did. "Fluently," Maria replied, having no idea what was happening.

Colonel Waldheim focused his attention on the emptying boxcars. "Sergeant," he called to the same sergeant. "What's taking so long?"

"Too many sick. They lay on the floor, and we cannot get them up. Typhus, sir. It's everywhere on this train."

"Anyone still in the boxcar who can't walk, shoot them," Waldheim said dispassionately. "They will soon die anyway." For him, the decision was not a difficult one, but one he made every day. He quickly turned back to Schrader and the woman. *She is very attractive,* he thought, eyes all over her. *The captain has good taste.*

They heard shooting from inside the boxcar. Maria jumped at the sound, but neither soldier looked up.

Maria said nothing but stood proud, her feet frozen to the cold ground, like the aristocrat they raised her to be. She felt their eyes on her and looked hard into the captain's eyes. Yes, she knew him. How could she ever forget him?

"Come here. Closer," Waldheim ordered. Maria obeyed.

After looking her over as he would a horse or cow, Waldheim reached down and raised her frock to her breasts. He admired her thin yet curvaceous body, fondled her as if by routine. Allowing the thin frock to fall back to cover her, he laughed. "Someone must have enjoyed you very much, Fraulein," he said, smiling with deviant pleasure to mock her.

Maria closed her eyes while he admired her nakedness, hoping in some way to block the humiliation. Captain Schrader, grimacing, fought to hold his emotions in check. Finally, Maria could take no more. She raised her head to look at the Colonel, and then she spat, striking the SS officer in the face.

Surprised by the insult, the spittle running down his cheek, he was unwilling to allow such defiance. He struck her hard across the face with the back of his hand. "She is another Austrian aristocrat who disobeys The Fuhrer," Waldheim hissed to Schrader. "She must be taught obedience, or she will try to escape." He looked sternly to the captain. "Beware, Schrader. I know them with their wealth and high manners. They are here, too. These traitors think the Americans will save them, so they spy on us."

Maria flinched but did not bow. A small streak of red trickled from her bruised lip.

"Wimmer deserves you, and, if we are fortunate, you will make the lives of those old Frenchmen miserable," he said without anger. "Captain, if she tries anything, if she is insubordinate, shoot her. I order it."

"Yes sir," Schrader replied, always the good subordinate, but he knew he had to get her away or Waldheim might shoot her on the spot. He looked around for his sergeant.

"Sergeant Schmidt," he called to his driver. "Take this prisoner and load her into the truck immediately. Restrain her."

"Yes, Herr Captain," Schmidt replied. He looked at Maria. "Come with me," he ordered.

Maria displayed no sign of fear as the SS sergeant led her away. She decided that anywhere was preferable to the horrible Dachau with its smells of death and its psychopathic leader.

Maria was unceremoniously loaded into a covered truck. Her hands were bound, but she was free to move about. *They know there is no place to run,* she decided, not knowing if she should feel relieved or fearful. She had no idea where they were taking her. But she believed that Kurt Schrader would not harm her wherever he was taking her.

Sergeant Schmidt did not speak while he bound and loaded her as if she were already dead. He was slim, stern of appearance, but his eyes startled her. Like the Gestapo, they were empty, dead, she decided.

She sat at the very end of the truck, looking for the last time at Dachau… she hoped. The cold mist sat heavy on the ground, dusting everything and everyone with its wetness. She watched the long lines of prisoners, men, women, and children. They seemed to be moving them toward the gate in the high barbwire fence.

Dogs barked and men yelled, but there was an eerie quiet among the prisoners.

Even the children know enough to be quiet, she thought.

The ride was long and bumpy. Six others traveled with her—all men—each bound like her. Kurt and the sergeant rode in front. Looking at the others, she saw they were all political prisoners like her, with their red triangles pinned to their breasts.

"Where are they taking us?" she asked the young man next to her.

"To our deaths, I suppose," was his only reply. No more words were spoken. When they reached their final destination, only Maria remained in the back.

She watched as each was off-loaded at a camp, all smaller facilities. In the growing light, she saw that the camps were teeming with people like the main Dachau camp.

The truck stopped and Schmidt came around to the back of the truck. "Get out," he ordered. He did not offer to assist her.

At last, my turn, she thought, her fear growing stronger. "Help me," she pleaded. "I cannot make it to the ground."

"Jump traitor," he again ordered, and Maria complied. She jumped awkwardly to the ground and fell on her side. He did not move but only watched her as she struggled to stand.

"Come," he said and dragged her brutishly by the arm. She felt pain as he pulled her along.

Maria quickly looked around. Not a camp like the others, she concluded. Looking up, she saw the high imposing castle wall rising in front of her. "What is this?"

"Shut up," Schmidt said, dragging her through a large wood double door. Captain Schrader had already entered and was standing in the middle of a very large room—a hall, she decided—and was talking to another soldier. The other soldier leered at her and smiled. Maria knew that look and hated the man instantly.

CHAPTER 3

April 28, 1945

Captain Jack Lee removed the unlit cigar from his mouth and spit, striking the main gun on the M4 Sherman tank he commanded. "What the hell he want a meeting for?" he asked his gunner, who had just returned from the Battalion command post. New orders, he figured, but did not say it.

"The major said he wants to meet with all the company commanders. Yup, that's what he says, Captain," Corporal Billy Minor replied. "Here's the mail. Just arrived from 12th Division." He reached up and handed a handful of letters to his commander.

"Thanks Billy. I'll hold a mail call, and then walk over to Kramer's tent to see what he wants." He quickly thumbed through the mail, searching for a letter. Finally, a letter from Anne. He smelled it and smiled. "She didn't forget me," he said softly so his men would not overhear. Those letters were the most important thing in the world to Jack Lee, and most of his men.

She had written once a week religiously since they landed at La Havre in November. Often it took time for the mail to catch up, but he always got at least one letter from home. His armored battalion was re-designated the 23rd just before they shipped out for Southampton, England. Across France to the Maginot line fortifications, the letters kept coming. The heavy fighting at Herrlisheim and the Vorges Mountains did not delay mail delivery, but everything slowed after they crossed the Rhine with Patton's Third Army on 21 March. Jack figured the mail carriers just lost track of the whereabouts of their battalion.

He could tell when someone didn't receive any mail for long periods. "Hard on morale, damn hard," he always said. He decided to make the meeting with Kramer before reading Anne's letter. He would savor it as long as he could.

Lee jumped off the tank, lit the cigar and sauntered over to the Major's tent. Along the way, he met up with another company commander serving in the 23rd Tank Battalion.

"Hey Lee, those tanks of yours on jet fuel?" John Sanders, commanding C Company, asked with a smile. "Company B rolls like you're headed direct to Vienna without stopping."

"Russians already took Vienna," Jack replied. "Don't you read your 'Stars and Stripes'?"

"I wonder who the Austrians think is worse—Hitler or Stalin."

"The faster we finish them all off, the best for everyone. Hit those Krauts hard and fast is the only way to end this thing and keep casualties down. And prevent Stalin's boys from overrunning all Europe."

Captain Sanders nodded and smiled.

When they arrived outside Major Kramer's tent, the other company commanders were already there. Kramer had set up a large tactical map of the area tied to the side of the GP small tent. The tall Texan waited patiently for all the commanders to gather in front of him. Kramer had been a schoolteacher in another life. Drafted in '42, he made the landing in North Africa and Normandy, and was reassigned to the 23rd in France before the big push to the Rhine. He was a survivor, had been around, and he knew it. So did his men.

Major Leonard Kramer, 23rd Tank Battalion, looked out over his audience and smiled. He thought he knew each man, had fought beside most of them since France. Seeing Lee and Sanders arrive, he prepared to speak:

"Gentlemen, we will prepare to move out tonight under darkness. Our recon has already left. Our objective is to cross into Austria and seize Kufstein. We got five days to do it, and we have to cross the Inn River before the SS blows the damn bridge. Got to hit them fast and hard. That's why I want Lee and B Company to lead all three tank companies into Austria. That understood?"

No one spoke but each man turned to look at Lee.

I also must inform you that we've been reassigned to the XXI Corps, the 36th Infantry Division. Get ready. I know your boys planned a rest after taking Landsberg Concentration camps. Sorry. Maybe at Kufstein. Any questions?"

Jack had hoped the battalion would stand down for a few days for a needed breather. He was tired and he understood that the war could end any day. He did not want to be the last American killed in "Krautland." With the 36th Infantry Division moving up quickly, he saw a brief glimmer of hope for a short respite. So much for that, he thought, as Kramer quickly brought him back to reality. Such are the demands of war. He knew his men would be disappointed and considered how to broach the subject. Directly, he decided quickly.

Sanders stepped forward to speak. "Major, what about the fuel train? Can they keep up?"

Kramer liked good tactical questions. "That's why we've been reassigned. The XXI Corps has that capability. Those Negro truck drivers are the best in the Division, and they never stop." He looked around, waiting. "Good. Then we drive for Austria."

Jack Lee stepped forward, pulled the cigar from his mouth and spit. "Major, if I may."

"Speak Captain."

"Our recon was getting interesting reports, mostly about the SS operations around here and in Austria. The locals, they don't tell us much, but there's this large prison camp. They call it Dachau, and it's huge with subcamps, bigger than the Landsberg Prison is, I hear. If we run into those, what do we do?"

"Depends on the resistance you get. If none, liberate it, free the prisoners, and hold the guards. That make sense?"

Jack spit. "Yeah, but if there's lots of prisoners… We don't have the logistics to take care of them. They're probably starving and need food and medical attention. The lousy Krauts. Do we let Division take care of them while we push on?"

The other commanders looked confused.

Major Kramer considered the question. It was an important one, he knew, and he decided he needed to explain further. "Open the gates, free all prisoners, capture the guards, and we'll get the Corps involved immediately, but keep moving toward your objective. That understood? The 36th Infantry will move in and wrap things up." He looked around at his men.

Everyone nodded. That made sense to them. Kramer seemed relieved. "Got it," Lee replied.

"And remember... Prepare your men for anything. We don't know what we may find, but it won't be good. We'll be up against a Panzer Division. 17th SS Panzers. They call themselves the Iron Fist."

"'Iron Fist' Why are they called that?"

"Hell, I don't know. Why they call us Hellcats?"

"Because we're tough, that's why," one of the commanders said.

"I'm sending along a demo team for the bridge," Kramer continued. "Remember: stop them from blowing that damn bridge."

"Yes, sir, understood," Lee said. "We'll be prepared. Hell, Major, we're always ready. You know that."

Kramer laughed along with the others. "Born ready, eh Captain?" He liked Captain Lee who he considered the most experienced tank commander he had. "The man has guts," he often quipped, having served as his commander since late November.

"Yup."

"Gentlemen, dismissed."

Both Sanders and Lee marched rapidly back to their company CPs. They had work to do, and Jack was anxious to read the letter from Anne.

When he returned to the tank he named "Besotten Jenny," his tank commanders had gathered to greet him. An informal bunch, no one saluted. They greeted him with "Jack" or "Captain Jack." The war was too long and hard for such military formalities.

"Boys, fuel up, load ammunition, and prepare to move out."

"Where to, Cap?" Andy Pride, his most senior commander asked. His voice reeked of disappointment. Andy had planned to catch up on his sleep. Jack knew him well.

"Boys, we're heading for Austria. Kufstein," Jack replied. "It'll take a couple of days at best, if we don't get bogged down at the Inn River. Stack up those C's. I don't know much about any resistance. "But I do know there's a Panzer unit called 'The Iron Fist' operating somewhere east of us. Heinrich Himmler's pride and joy, and they got Tigers. I hope the war ends before we run into them. Any questions?"

There was none. Everything seemed routine for his men. They had been doing it for months now, but no one liked the idea of confronting Panzers. Each man returned to his tank. They needed to quickly brief their crews and prepare to move out.

Jack sat down on the turret of Besotten Jenny to read his letter from home. A slight mist filled the air. Not like in West Texas, he thought.

He carefully opened the envelope after smelling it. The best part. Unfolding the many pages, he read:

My dearest Jack…

He smiled, pulled out a new cigar, bit off the end and lit up. Through the course of the letter, Jack smiled, frowned, and laughed. Finally, he wiped away a tear.

He thought about his young son—less than a year old. "James," he whispered. He had never met him, the baby being born two months after he shipped out for England. He wondered if he were killed, what would happen to them. When the war finally ended, and he returned to them and civilian life, would things work out? Could he support them? The nearer the end of the war, the more he worried. Those thoughts ran through his mind like a raging torrent of water.

He raised his head, forced away his thoughts and anxieties, and tried to focus. Hey, we got ourselves a mission, he told himself. Get your head right, soldier.

Bravo Company was ready to move out within an hour. The tankers fired up their engines and waited for their captain in Besotten Jenny.

Jack stood and looked behind him. The Shermans were lined up and ready to go, he saw. "Good, good," he said with a smile. "Now, we wait for the sun to set."

"Move out!" Jack called, standing on the turret of his tank in the gathering twilight. He faced behind him and raised his arm high for everyone to see. Then he dropped it to signal, "Move out." His tank growled forward, with dark fumes rising into the cool air. Slowly, the column moved forward down the road and out of the meadow. Single file behind Besotten Jenny, they headed southeast toward Austria.

His tank column reached the Inn River bridge around midnight. Jack halted the column well away from the old iron structure.

"Bring up the demo team," he radioed back.

A six-man team headed by an NCO arrived at his tank within minutes. "Yes, sir," the sergeant said to Jack, who had jumped to the ground.

"Now's your shot, Sergeant Grimm," Jack said with a smile. "Check those trusses real close. The Krauts are clever."

"No problem, sir. We've done this before," Grimm replied with a salute off the top of his helmet. "Let's go, boys," he called to the remainder of his team behind him. "Shouldn't take long, Cap'n."

"I'm sending a platoon with you to provide security. They'll spread out on the other side," Jack said, turning back. "Bring up Sergeant Glenn," he called.

The Black sergeant jumped out of the front of a truck carrying the infantry and stood in front of Lee. "Yeah suh," he said with a sloppy salute.

"Glenn, take a platoon and deploy to the other side of the bridge. The demo boys need some security."

"Yeah suh," Glenn replied. "Let's go boys." He waved to the truck and two dozen men jumped out.

"Other side," Glenn ordered, and everyone ran across the bridge. Demo team members split off as they crossed. They figured any explosives had to be tied to the uprights for maximum effect.

Quiet reigned around the bridge while the noise of the idling tanks disturbed the tranquility behind Lee. He paced, constantly checking his watch. Then, breaking the quiet, he heard a yell from under the bridge.

"Found one, all wired and ready," a man called from directly below in the cross frames. "Hey, here's another," the same man called.

"Hurray, cut those wires and throw the damn things in the river," Grimm told him from the top of the bridge.

Suddenly small arms fire exploded from the tree line on the far side. Grimm dived to the road. A machine gun opened up.

"Not ours," Jack said to his tank commander. Then he heard M1s fire. He hoped all his men had found cover. A brief firefight ensued. Finally, quiet again.

"Got a couple more over here, Sarge," another of Grimm's men called out. "You know what to do with it."

Grimm heard the splashes of the explosives hitting the water. "Good," he said. "Charlie, you think that's all of 'em?"

Before Charlie could reply, an explosion rocked the far bank of the river. "Shit," Jack mumbled. "What the hell?" he called to Grimm, still belly to the ground on the bridge. He did not respond.

Glenn's men had begun to sweep the area outward from their earlier positions but met no further resistance.

"Hey, don't worry," Charlie called from under the bridge. "I just missed the water, and the damn thing musta hit a tree."

The remainder of the demo team crawled up the riverbank to the bridge. Each gave the all-clear sign to Grimm.

Grimm waved to Jack.

"Get ready to move out," Jack ordered his tank commander, who gave the signal to the others via their radio.

CHAPTER 4

May 2, 1945
Schloss Itter (Castle), Tyrol, Austria

Itter was built around 1240 in the mountains of western Austria in a remote location, surrounded by deep forests and white peaks. The castle, dominating the surrounding area, was not constructed in a single week or even in a single year. By its appearance and design, it had taken hundreds of workers many months if not years to construct and reconstruct.

Itter, during its long history, served many masters and served many different functions from military, administrative, and finally, a household. Initially built to serve the counts and Bishops of Regensburg, it was sold to Archbishop Pilgrim II of Salzburg in 1380. Eventually the stone walls housed a North Tyrolean administrative facility.

In 1524-1525, heavy fighting during the German Peasants Revolt in and around the Tyrol saw Schloss Itter devastated. It lay in ruins for more than four hundred years, the great granite walls protecting its emptiness and solitude in the mountains, forests, and pastures of the area. Not until 1878 did the castle rise again from the empty ruins of its destruction. Artisans and workmen from the region painstakingly rebuilt the walls and interior, restoring it to its thirteenth century splendor.

Sofie Menter, pianist, composer, and student of Franz Liszt, purchased the castle in 1884 as a residence. Numerous musical productions were held there featuring the well-known musicians of the day. She sold it in 1902, and Itter was remodeled, passing through several hands before the Nazis took possession.

The Third Reich commandeered the well-built stone fortress eventually to hold high-ranking and mostly French political prisoners.

The Nazis, when they annexed Austria in 1938, were attracted to Castle Itter by its remote location, deep moats, and massive stone construction. Berlin requisitioned it for official use when the war began. In 1943, Heinrich Himmler's SS took over the castle grounds with all its outbuildings as a detention facility for prisoners they considered potentially valuable and placed it under the operational control of the concentration command at Dachau, with its 123 satellite facilities in southern Germany and northern Austria. Funding, guards, and support came directly from the main camp.

The commandant insisted that Maria, when she first arrived, learn the name of each "guest." Maria never understood why since they like her were all prisoners of the Third Reich. But she followed orders obediently and quickly memorized their name and rank.

Edouard Daladier, former prime minister of France; General Maurice Gamelin, former chief of staff of the French Army; his successor, General Maxime Weygand; Paul Reynaud, former premier of France; tennis star Jean Borotra; rightwing leader, Colonel Francois de La Rocque; Michel Clemenceau, politician and son of the World War I Prime Minister; Andre Francois-Poncet, former French ambassador to Italy; Leon Jouhaux, trade union leader; Agnes Cailliau, sister of Free French leader Charles De Gaulle and her husband, politician Alfred Cailliau. Each made a point to tell her repeatedly how important to France he was before defeat and capture by the Germans.

The victorious Germans also incarcerated their wives, Reynaud's young secretary, Christiane Mabire, and Jouhaux's secretary, Madame Brucklin. The Germans reconstructed twenty rooms in the old castle as cells to hold them.

Maria became friends with the other four inmates sent from Dachau to serve the prisoners. They were two cooks—Andre and Pierre, who she learned were French Jews. The other servant, Bridget, also a Jew, was a schoolgirl from Berlin. The handyman, Czech, Andre Cuckovic, seemed inscrutable to her, but was also the friendliest. Of the VIPs, she felt only former premier, Paul Reynaud, treated her like a human being, and not as their scullery servant.

The VIPs disliked each other immensely. Maria immediately noticed the constant tension and disregard they openly expressed for others of a different political persuasion, and they often divided into ideological camps when together. They rarely spoke to each other, and if they did, it often ended in heated disagreement.

Each—servant and VIP—knew they could be executed at any time by their German masters, and it was something everyone discussed openly. Their concern for surviving united them, but at the same time, each understood that life at Castle Itter was still much better than in the camps.

Everyone was also aware from talk among the guards that the Russians and Americans were getting close, and that soon the war would finally end. Each wondered if they could hold out until that happened. Fear of an unknown and dangerous future came to shroud every conversation as May fast approached.

"Maria, you must do as I say, or Commandant Wimmer will have you shot."

"The man is unfit for command," she replied.

"Even so, we must keep the faith. The Americans will arrive soon," Captain Schrader said softly to the young woman. "I've heard that Captain Martin Weiß, who commands at Dachau, will come here if the Americans don't get him first. He's worse than Wimmer."

"Impossible. He can't be any worse than Wimmer. I would rather die than let that vile drunk touch me. You should have let me die at Dachau."

"Because I love you, have always loved you since the day my father brought you into our home," Kurt pleaded. He grabbed his cane to get closer to her. "Here, we have the best chance to survive this horrible war, but we must be watchful."

He tried to kiss her, but Maria broke free of his embrace. "No Kurt, stop," she replied, stepping back. "I am married to your half-brother. You know that," she reminded him. "And I am your prisoner here."

"Josef, where is he? Who knows? Probably dead, along with thousands of others. When was the last you heard from him?"

"Last fall. Oh, I don't remember. So much has happened."

Kurt looked at her, trying to understand. He thought he knew her, a simple girl who desired to marry an aristocrat—a prince. She had it all—passion, beauty, and good sense. The woman standing here now he did not know. "Why? Why did you commit treason, Maria? You could have fled west as a refugee toward the Americans."

"Oh Kurt, you think I am just some simple country girl, and perhaps six years ago, I was, but I've changed, we've all changed. So much death, everything destroyed. What does it mean?"

"I don't have an answer. Hitler... we hoped, believed."

"Don't you see? I had to do something—anything—for my own sanity. The horrors... the bombings, the Gestapo watching us. I could not stand by," she said, suddenly feeling free to express her feelings, or not caring any longer. "An American pilot, his plane was shot down. We found him on the estate. I could not let him die."

"You protected him, shielded him from the Home Guard. If they had not known of your connection to our family and feared Father, they would have shot you in the village square. Colonel Waldheim told me this."

"That pig," she hissed angrily. "He's evil just like the Gestapo."

Kurt closed his eyes to gather his thoughts. "Here, Maria, I can protect you, but you must be careful of what you say, even to the French. You must understand that."

Maria closed her eyes and then shook her head. "Oh Kurt, I cannot continue the charade. I hate the Nazis, have always hated them. I hate them for what they did to you. Where is my husband? Dead somewhere in an unmarked grave in France?" Her worry for her husband extracted a toll on her. She was unable to control her emotions, even knowing she was speaking with an SS officer as well as a childhood friend. She realized it was becoming increasingly difficult to keep Kurt at arm's length.

"War, Maria, war. You are not the only one who has lost. My father and Josef dead, we have only each other." He watched her, feeling engulfed by love. "That is the way it is."

She looked at his uniform, at the lightening runes on his collar, and that reminded her of to whom she was speaking. "No Kurt, that is gone, too," she replied coldly. "You are no different from Wimmer or the others, and I am condemned as a spy."

"Maria, the war will soon end, and I cannot predict what will happen to any of us, but surrendering to the Americans must be better than the Russians."

"Josef is not dead. I must believe. It is all I believe." She knew she had to hold on to that, if only for her own sanity.

The commandant, Captain Sebastian Wimmer entered the room off the kitchen where they were speaking. "What is this? The prisoners must be fed." He looked hard at Maria. "Go or I will punish you harshly."

Maria ran from the room and Wimmer turned his attention to Kurt. "Captain Schrader, you serve here at my pleasure. If you do not follow my

orders, I will send you back to your unit, which is probably retreating from the Bolsheviks as we speak. Do you understand?"

"I understand. I will attend to security." He turned to disappear into the darkness of the castle, but Wimmer had more to say to him.

"Captain, I know it's been a while since you had a woman, but I warn you.

That one is mine."

Kurt said nothing, trying to walk away. Hate for Wimmer, his superior officer, began to burn deep, and with Wimmer's interest in Maria, he knew he had to protect her even from him. *How will I handle that?* he asked himself.

In the large main hall, Maria and Bridget waited on their guests. There was little food to provide them with—carrots and potatoes—but the ritual continued. They poured wine, still plentiful in the castle stores, and fed them their meager rations. But, she wondered, when the food is almost gone, who will eat and who will starve? That became the primary topic of conversation among the servants. Each knew the answer but did not speak of it.

Andre Poncet, the former ambassador, abruptly waved at Bridget. "Yes, Monsieur Ambassador?"

"Coffee, bring me coffee. I want it now," he demanded.

Bridget ran into the kitchen and quickly returned with a filled cup. "Monsieur, coffee."

She set it down on the table in front of the diplomat, bowed politely, and stepped back.

Poncet sipped from the cup. He then made a strange gurgling noise and spit out the remainder on the floor beside his feet. "Ugh, what is this? Jewess, are you trying to poison me? This is not even chicory."

Frightened, Bridget stammered, "No monsieur, it is not chicory. We have no more."

"I demand you tell me what it is."

"We are using acorns. It is all that we have."

The others listened to the conversation. General Weygand, sitting across the table from Poncet finally grew tired of the Fascist ambassador. "Monsieur, shut up. We are lucky they don't shoot us or starve us. Be satisfied."

"Monsieur General, this is completely unsatisfactory. A Jewess who deserves to die in the camps serves us. What is this? Poison?" Poncet grabbed Bridget's arm, pulled up her sleeve to expose a camp tattoo. "See this?" He held up Bridget's arm for everyone to see.

"We have no more chicory so I must use crushed acorns," a frightened Bridget exclaimed to everyone gathered at the table, as if pleading her case in court.

Maria could take no more from the fascist. "What do you want from us, monsieur? All are trying to survive the best we can, and we make no decisions here. If you are unhappy, talk to the commandant."

Poncet stood and prepared to leave the table.

"Yes, leave her alone, monsieur traitor. You are nothing but a demented fascist," General Weygand said. "Did you upset your buddy, Himmler? Is that why you are here with the rest of us?"

"Go to hell," Poncet fired back.

At this point in their heated exchange, Madame Cailliau spoke, "Gentlemen, civility please. We are wasting valuable time. We must focus on surviving this horrid place."

Poncet looked at her with contempt. "Madame, do you expect your brother, the great general to rescue us?"

"You… I do not know, but my brother is doing his duty to France with great courage." She looked around the table while speaking, knowing that several at the table did not agree.

The hall suddenly grew silent. Each guest tried to focus mostly on drink. The servants retreated to the sanctity of the kitchen, while the four SS guards, watching them, kept their distance, not caring about their conversations.

All heard the pounding of artillery and tank fire in the far distance. Each— prisoner and guard—contemplated its meaning.

Darkness soon engulfed the castle and its varied cast of characters. The war was inching closer to Castle Itter and the nearby village of Worgl, six miles away. The Wehrmacht were retreating from the Russians in the east and the Americans and British from the west. Trapped between two great advancing armies, time was running short for the Third Reich. Foremost on every prisoner's mind was who would liberate them, or if the SS would shoot them before they were liberated. Each immediately understood they were completely vulnerable to the shifting fortunes of war, and what they did not know was quickly supplanted by rumor.

Maria stood on the ramparts, her work completed for the day, and gazed out at the night sky. To the north and west, she saw flashes of light and an occasional boom, boom of artillery. She worried about Josef. She always fretted about her husband, wondering if he were still alive and fighting or dead somewhere in an unmarked grave.

CHAPTER 5

Joaquin Speers, Major, Schutzstaffel, Sixth Waffen SS Panzer Army, commanded what remained of his battalion—three Tiger tanks and about 150 men. His battalion, the advance, of the 3rd Panzergrenadier Division, had engaged with Tolbukhin's Third Ukrainian Front since early February of '45, having fought well, but overwhelmed by sheer numbers.

They had been on the Eastern Front since early 1943, successfully recapturing Kharkov and had fought heroically at Kursk. The Division went on the defense at Warsaw, and in Hungary. Following a failed March offensive, the Red Army forced them to the outskirt of Vienna. Following bitter fighting around the city, they had to retreat across Austria. The entire third Panzer Division had only six tanks and 1,000 men remaining. Yet, the war continued.

He recently received word that Hitler was dead, having taken his own life in a bunker in Berlin. For some reason, that did not surprise him. He was not the type to surrender, especially to the Russians, nor would he flee. Where would he go?

The SS now commanded the armies in Austria, and his orders he was determined to follow until he was killed or forced to surrender. Speers heard rumors that Himmler was attempting to make a separate peace with the Americans. But, after further thought, he scoffed at the idea. Why should the Americans bargain with him? he wondered.

He knew Himmler personally, and did not like the man, but he admired his spirit. "We must fight on until the end," Himmler wrote to all his commanders and their lieutenants. "We will follow a scorched earth policy," he ordered. Speers smiled. Hell, we've been doing that since the Ukraine, he thought.

We took a sacred oath to defend the Reich to our last breath. Now, we are asked to do just that. He thought of his wife, his Emma. She was killed only months earlier in our apartment in Berlin by the Bolshevik bombers. My son killed at Stalingrad.

All have given their lives for the Third Reich, he thought. I am proud of our sacrifices. Himmler noted them earlier by special accommodation that he wore close to his heart.

Is it now my turn? He tried to remain resolute, but the end was close at hand. He held Himmler's final order in his hand. Not far from his thoughts was the action he personally would take when the war was finally over. Surrender or flee? He knew his best chance was with the Americans, but even then, he did not know how they would treat him.

Soldiering was all Major Speers knew. "I've lived and I'll die a soldier," he often vowed to friends and colleagues. "I follow orders. I give orders. Whatever they are. This is the routine I have always lived by, where I feel most comfortable. As a man, that is who I am. I fight and if necessary, I will die, but I will die as a proud German soldier." Few doubted his words.

Speers stood in the middle of the road looking at his remaining tanks. The Division had 3,000 tanks at Kursk and now he had only three with one assault gun. He was happy to have three. Several of the battalions had none remaining.

He halted their advance. Heavy cover provided by dense forests protected him from strafing from American planes, but the thousands of fleeing refugees that clogged the roads still hindered movement west.

He reread Himmler's orders for the third time.

Move to Schloss Itter, take and hold it against the American advance. Handle the mess regarding prisoners quickly and expeditiously.

Major Speers knew immediately what that meant. He had been doing it since the invasion of the USSR. His men were few, but his major concern was the war could be over before he reached Itter. With Hitler dead, he did not know how long Germany's armies would hold out before he would be compelled to surrender. Days, perhaps a couple of weeks at most, he thought.

His commanders, as few as they were, gathered around him for the latest briefing. "Be prepared to move out. I have ordered a platoon of infantry to clear the roads of refugees so that we can pass," he ordered. "We will advance to Schloss Itter. I have received intelligence that indicates the Americans will seize Kuftstein and will push toward Innsbruck west of the castle." Would it be their final battle? He already knew the answer, as did his men.

"Herr Major," Captain Wolfgang Meier, one of his captains called out above the noise. He stepped forward. "Where are we going? We are surrounded. The Russians are behind us, and the Americans in front. Should we not surrender and plead for good terms?"

"Good terms? What are good terms, Captain? A prison camp or perhaps, they will give all of us to the Russians. Do you think you can survive there? They will shoot you."

"Understood, Herr Major," Meier replied. The other men in the circle looked at each other, as if they thought things would never come to this.

"We have fought well. The Death Head Division will be remembered. At Budapest, the Russians took heavy casualties and had to bring up more divisions to stop us."

"But what do we have left? Three tanks and 150 tired soldiers. That is all, Herr Major," another of his commanders said. "What can we do at this old castle?"

"We are ordered to take Schloss Itter, prepare its defenses, and wait for the American army to arrive," Speers replied immediately. He was determined to carry out this final order. "It is a prison, part of Dachau and holds prisoners. We must deal with them. Does everyone understand?"

Except for one man, each nodded that he understood. Captain Meier stepped forward to pose another question. "Sir is Himmler even alive?" he asked. "Or perhaps he is on his way to South America."

At hearing the question, the others forced back a chuckle. Speers could see what was written on each face. Casual indifference and humor breed defeat, he thought.

"Captain, your question borders on insubordination. It is not your concern where your commanding officer is. The war continues and I expect you to do your duty. Is that understood?"

"Ja, Herr Major," Meier replied.

"Gentlemen, our final battle for the Third Reich." The officers cheered, but half-heartedly at best.

"We have fought with great honor. We will die with great honor," Speers shouted proudly. "Go to your men. We will move out at sunset."

Slowly and with indiscriminate brutality, the infantry platoon forced hundreds of refugees to the side of the road. Most were old men, women, and children. They carried bundles on their backs or pushed simple hand carts filled with their meager belongings. Speers heard sporadic gunfire, but he was indifferent to its meaning. He was completely absorbed in executing his final mission.

When darkness approached, his remaining three tanks started. Their engines rumbled to life. Each crew knew that fuel reserves were gone, and they had to achieve their final objective on what they had in their tanks.

"Move out!" Major Speers called to his troops. The armored beasts slowly moved forward with infantry riding forward and aft of the tanks. The column passed through the narrow corridor of refugees opened by his infantry, having forced many distraught civilians deeper into the forest.

Those refugees remaining on the road watched as they passed. Speers saw the contempt written on their faces. He felt it. The fear the SS had generated in earlier days had evaporated. Now, they only feared the Russians, for what they could do to them as citizens of the Third Reich.

CHAPTER 6

Captain Wimmer, like Major Speers, also pondered his own fate. The enemy was closing in. Do I surrender or flee? Questions he had considered regularly for weeks now. While in Vienna, he had consulted a fortuneteller. She told him he would live a long life, but he was not so certain. Each day their situation grew more difficult with food stocks precariously low and the enemy closing in on all sides.

He was a Bavarian, not married, so he had no family with which to concern himself. The French killed his father at Verdun in the First World War. Mother, dear old Mama, he thought. She lived in Nuremberg where he had grown up. He had not visited her in several years, even though the trip was short. He rarely wrote her. Their relationship quickly deteriorated after the SS recruited him. He wanted to serve his Fuhrer the best way he could. Mama never understood, he thought with feelings of indifference toward her. Wimmer had no siblings. His only friends quickly became other SS soldiers.

Few would describe him as good looking, balding, and short, with dark eyes. He looked upon Captain Schrader with envy bordering on hate. He was the perfect Aryan—tall, blond, and much better educated. Wimmer's mother, despite being working class and not high-titled, sent him to the best Catholic schools in Bavaria. She could not afford college for her only child, as times were very bad until Hitler saved Germany.

The SS were the brothers he never had. He relished that comradery and sense of family offered by the brotherhood. That is, until his assignment to guard French prisoners in Itter Castle. It was a dead-end assignment, he had always known that, but the contempt he received from others he served with who were fighting on the fronts bothered him greatly. Forgotten and ignored, isolated in the Austrian Alps, he drank heavily to bury the humiliation, and even scorn he received from his brothers. That was what he blamed his heavy drinking on when someone asked, but no one did.

"Bring me the Austrian woman," he ordered one of his guards. He reached over to pour himself schnapps. He had been drinking most of the day. The best part of the job, he thought. *All the wine and schnapps I can drink at no cost.*

"Which woman, Herr Captain?" the guard asked.

Wimmer looked at him as if he had asked a very stupid question. He flopped back down in his chair and sipped his drink. "You fool!" he growled. "The beauty from Vienna, not the Jewess."

"Ja, Herr Captain." The young private ran from the room.

The private is new and very young, Wimmer thought, watching him leave. *The war… Now, we must scrape the bottom of the barrel for good men—children they send us.* He shook his head.

Shortly, the young private returned with Maria in tow. Wimmer watched her enter. She still wore the harsh cotton shift, but she had begun to fill it out. He saw her breasts and buttocks pressing against the worn and flimsy garment. Her hair, a deep rich, natural blond was returning. The scars and bruises had healed.

He stood to greet her.

Maria pushed his hand away and stood glowering at Wimmer. "What do you want?" she hissed at him.

"Leave us, Private," he said, looking at the young woman.

"Ja, Herr Captain," the boy said, turned and quickly departed the room.

Wimmer walked around the desk, not too steady on his feet. The drink was having an effect. He stopped in front of Maria again, so close she felt his breath on her face. "You are happy here, da? For that you owe me, I think."

Maria said nothing but stepped back from him. She easily smelled alcohol.

Wimmer had been attracted to her from the first time he saw her getting out of the truck from Dachau. Now is the right moment, he'd decided, watching her serve the French earlier in the day.

To possess her. That was the single thought driving him at that moment. He reached out to grab her around the waist with both hands.

Maria tried to push them away.

Wimmer saw the fear in her eyes, and he bathed in it. The Jewess, Bridget, meekly gave in to his sexual demands. Too easy, he thought. He found the young prisoners exciting, arousing especially when they struggled. He loved the feel of power surging through his body when they fought him.

This woman he gave special treatment—extra rations, even an occasional bath, to make her more desirable.

"Let go of me… please," she screamed.

He put his mouth against her lips. She bit his lower lip and pushed him away. "You're drunk, Herr Captain. Don't touch me," she demanded, fighting to escape him.

Just as he hoped. The power he felt surged through his body. It gave him an erection. He spat blood, forming where she bit him.

She knew she was no match, and that his strength could overpower her.

"Who are you to bark orders to me?" He trapped her against the old desk, and then reached down with both hands to raise her frock to her breasts. She was naked under the frock. He leered drunkenly at her nakedness.

She reached for anything to stop him, but there was nothing.

With her frock still raised, Wimmer spun her around and forced her to face the desk. He placed both hands on her breasts. "Now, you will know what it's like to be fucked by a real man. I will get what I'm owed." Pinning her tightly against the desk, he unbuttoned his pants.

"Let me go. I demand that you free me," she said, struggling frantically against his superior strength. She felt him against her buttocks. "Help! Help me!" she called out.

The door flew open just as Wimmer prepared to penetrate her. Captain Schrader charged into the room on his cane. He held a Luger in his hand. "You swine," he hissed. "Get off her."

Wimmer pulled back, surprised by the unexpected intrusion from one of his own men. He immediately put his penis back in his pants, staggered slightly on his feet, and turned to face Schrader. "What? Get out! Now!"

Maria stood straight and modestly pulled her frock down to cover herself. She then gave Wimmer a hard shove. She felt outraged, embarrassed, and violated, at the same time. When the Gestapo officer did this in March, she swore she wanted to die, but now, she wanted to kill this man. "Shoot him. Do it now, Kurt," she demanded. "Give me the gun. I will do it."

Kurt looked at her, and then at Wimmer. He held his weapon on his commanding officer, but quickly, his anger turned to confusion. "Maria, I…"

"He was going to rape me. Shoot him."

"You're nothing but a common gutter pig," Kurt said to Wimmer. "When they finally arrive, I'll see that you're punished for this. Shot like the rabid dog you are."

Kurt still held his weapon but lowered it slowly. The moment for shooting Wimmer had passed.

"Kurt, he tried to violate me, the Nazi pig," she said, her fury barely contained. "Shoot him."

"No," he said, unable to look at her. Watching Wimmer, he saw that he was severely intoxicated.

Wimmer slowly staggered back to his chair and slumped down hard, his trousers still unbuttoned. He laughed. "A traitor, Captain, a spy who should have been shot. She is mine to do with as I please. Get out!"

"You're drunk. Leave her alone."

"I could have you both shot. On my order, a guard will enter and take you out back and shoot you."

"No, Captain Wimmer, you will not."

"Captain Schrader, when the battalion arrives, I will have you shot with the rest of them. All of them, those snooty Frenchies and the prisoners."

"Where is Captain Weiß, where is Himmler? They are running or dead."

"They are close, Captain, and they have orders to take this place. No one will survive, not even you. A traitor to the Fatherland like the woman."

Maria had enough. She no longer cared what happened. She turned and marched out of the room, not knowing or caring where she should go.

The two men, still confronting each other, turned to watch as she stormed out the door. "Get out of my quarters, Captain Schrader, or I'll have you both shot now."

Kurt turned to face Wimmer one more time. "You were very lucky today that I did not shoot you, Herr Captain. Tomorrow, I may change my mind."

He left Wimmer's room still holding his Lugar. He returned to his room on a higher floor in the castle now realizing what he had done. He entered, locked the door, and lay down on the single cot. He rested the weapon on his chest for quick action if needed.

He did not plan to sleep but tried to think through the events of the evening. The night was late, and he was exhausted. Wimmer deserved to die, he thought, but not by my hand. He worried that Maria's honor should have been avenged. Was he a coward for not shooting a rapist, or a good soldier for allowing his commanding officer to live? The question haunted him.

Captain Wimmer stared at the empty bottle of schnapps sitting on his desk.

He knew he was drunk, very drunk.

"I am in command here," he said loudly to no one. "Schrader is nothing and must be gotten rid of. The woman, too, if she does not submit to me." He staggered to the door, opened it and walked into the main hall.

"Guards," he called. "Where the hell are my guards?"

Sergeant Schmidt entered the hall from the courtyard. "Ja, Herr Captain," he said. "What do you want?"

"More schnapps. I must have more schnapps," he slurred and staggered to the nearest chair. "Get some."

"There is no more, Herr Captain," Schmidt replied. "We have wine."

"Schnapps, Sergeant, and now," Wimmer ordered.

"I will look, Herr Captain," Schmidt said. "I will send someone to the village." "If you must then do it, Sergeant."

Without another word, Schmidt left the room.

CHAPTER 7

Sporadic gunfire on the outskirts of Worgl, six miles from Castle Itter, echoed up the mountain. A dozen soldiers commanded by Major Josef Gangl fired at partisan snipers hidden inside the village.

The snipers and soldiers were Austrians, the soldiers having served in the 19th Field Army. Although composed primarily of conscripts, and wounded veterans from other units, the Army's different battalions had fought valiantly. Originally assigned to defend southern France, they later fought in the Vosges Mountains, Alsace, Baden, and southern Wurttemberg, in a strategic retreat from the Allied advance. During Operation Dragoon, the 19th was almost completely destroyed as a fighting force, having suffered 7,000 killed, 20,000 wounded and 135,000 captured. They rebuilt the 19th Army, and the Americans destroyed it yet again in the battle of Colmar Pocket. Defending the approach to the Rhine River, they suffered huge losses, but again, the 19th was rebuilt. The end for the division came in heavy fighting around the area of Stuttgart in late April 1945.

Major Gangl, himself a conscript, was a battalion commander with the 105th Infantry Brigade. The fighting at Stuttgart decimated his command, leaving himself, another officer, and twelve soldiers in his battalion. Without higher authority or direction, they were left on their own. The men, with Gangl's quiet support, retreated toward home, all believing the war had to end soon.

When one of Gangl's men spotted a target in the village, usually in a second story window, he fired off a round, and so the firefight went. Neither side gaining an advantage, yet neither forced to submit.

"Herr Major, they have us pinned down," Lieutenant Wolf Freerland said. "The fire is coming from that street." He pointed in the direction of the sniper fire. "But I don't think there are many." Rounds zipped over their heads.

Gangl considered the situation. "Show them a white flag. We will talk with them first. With Hitler dead, the war will soon end, and we must not risk lives unnecessarily."

Josef Gangl had been at war since 1941 when conscripted. He was tired, tired of the death and destruction, but mostly at seeing the horrible suffering surrounding him. Germans, French, Americans, it did not matter any longer. Since the summer of 1944, they had retreated from southern France to the Rhine, and finally into Germany and Austria.

The fighting had been bitter. They had suffered many casualties. From the battalion he commanded, only these men remained. The others killed, wounded or deserted. What's the point? he thought, watching men disappear at night under cover of darkness. At some point, families—protecting children, a wife, elderly parents—had to take precedent over Adolf Hitler's Third Reich.

Josef, only 26 but feeling already very old, had a clever mind for warfare, and proved courageous under fire. Handsome in a rugged way, he was a natural leader. Men looked up to him, and he quickly rose through the ranks, facilitated by a very high casualty rate in his infantry unit.

Since arriving in France, his unit was part of General der Infanterie Weise's Army, but each time the Army reorganized due to heavy losses, his battalion was re-named, with a different commander. The most recent Army Group Commander was Erich Brandenberger, General der Panzertruppe.

Along the Rhine, they fought first against Patton's Third Army and then to hold off Devers'. By late April, they became so few they had no choice but to withdraw from the field or face capture. He knew, as did most of his soldiers, that the war was lost months earlier. After the "great" Ardennes offensive failed, it seemed too futile to fight on. It was only a matter of days before the Army Command surrendered, he knew, and his men knew. Everyone easily saw that the Third Reich was collapsing around them.

"Ja, Herr Major, but the men sir... ?" Lieutenant Freerland said. "The men?"

"They talk, sir. They say it is time to surrender and go home. Many plan to desert."

The two men walked cautiously toward the village, to where his men dug in. He surveyed the area with its ancient trees and upper open windows. Immediately behind his soldiers, Josef greeted an older soldier, Sergeant Willy Krouse, the ranking NCO. "Sergeant, spread the word. We will attempt to talk with them to arrange a truce. To go on fighting is futile," Josef said.

"Then, your orders, Herr Major?" Krouse asked.

"Send a man forward under a flag of truce. Arrange a cease fire and I will speak to their leader."

"Ja, Herr Major," Krouse replied, but hesitated. He gave his commander a strange look.

"What is it?" Josef saw immediately that something was bothering him. After months together in combat, they knew each other well.

"The war is finished, sir. The men want to go home now. Some prepare to leave tonight, to desert."

"Too dangerous to go off on your own. An SS Battalion is near; partisans fight in the woods and prey on soldiers wandering off. If a soldier is captured by the SS fleeing for home, he will be shot as a deserter. We must stay together as a unit if only to protect ourselves, Sergeant. Convince them."

"Ja, Herr Major, I will convince them."

"Thank you, Sergeant Krouse. Dismissed." Krouse saluted the two officers with pride. Relieved, he returned to his men.

Soon, a white cloth tied to a Mauser waved in the direction of the village. Two men held it high for everyone in the village to see. Ten minutes later, they saw a white flag waved from inside the doorway of a house several blocks into the village.

Sergeant Krouse and one of his men walked carefully down the cobblestone street, the white flag held high over Krouse's head, as he neared the doorway. Two men exited the house and walked toward them. Dressed in civilian clothes, Krouse observed two partisans armed only with pistols. A short conversation ensued, ending with nods on both sides. When the conversation ended, Sergeant Krouse waved to Major Gangl and Lieutenant Freerland.

"Stay Lieutenant. It may be a trick. If I don't return, command them. Take the village and hold it. Surrender only to the Americans."

"Ja Major."

Josef walked toward the four men. They met in the middle of the street where men from both sides were able to observe. The partisan leader greeted Josef with a cold nod. "I am Charles Stein, with the Austrian resistance. With whom am I speaking?"

"I am Major Josef Gangl," he replied, declining to offer a unit designation. He did not know if the 19th even existed any longer, so what did it matter? "Who are you?"

"We are the resistance—the Salzkammergut. We were trained in Slovenia to free Austria of you. Some are Jews, many Catholics, but most are communists returning from Moscow. We even have a monarchist among us, and there are those like yourself, perhaps… deserters." He searched Gangl's face for a reaction.

"We are not deserters but Austrians like you," Josef replied testily.

"I understand, Major. Many soldiers are joining our ranks, and that is good. We need your experience and, of course, good German weapons to use on good Nazis, eh?"

"Is this your village, Stein?"

Stein smiled. "Ha! We live mostly in the forest. That way it is easier and safer to blow bridges and trains until the Americans arrive. I think they will arrive very soon."

"What of the castle?" He pointed up the mountain.

"French prisoners held by the Nazis," Stein replied. "When the Americans arrive, we will liberate them… we hope." The last comment was telling.

"Are there many?"

"Not many, but the walls are high." Stein quickly grew impatient of the banter. "Major, what do you wish to discuss?"

"Since the war will soon be over, there is no longer a need to kill each other. We—all of us—can wait out the arrival of the Americans. My men wish only to stay here and surrender when they arrive. Do you understand?"

"I understand. Will you disarm?"

"We will surrender and disarm only to the Americans. I ask for a truce until that time."

Stein considered the offer. Both men knew the Americans would arrive in a few days, and here at least in Worgl, the war would be over.

"If your men create no problems in Worgl, we will not fire on you, but understand, you will be watched closely."

Josef nodded his agreement. "I accept those terms."

"Major, we have learned that an SS Panzer armored battalion is moving toward us and is close to the castle, so beware. I think they have different plans than surrendering to the Americans."

"Thank you for agreeing to a truce… and for the intelligence."

Seeing the two enemies standing in the street and appearing to negotiate under a flag of truce was a good sign for Burgermeister Herr Gustov Herring. Hesitating at first, he soon departed his cottage nearby and walked out to the two. He wore his Nazi armband.

"Gentlemen, I am Gustov Herring, Burgermeister of Worgl," he said extending his hand to each man. There was no saluting of any kind.

They shook hands. The two armed combatants waited impatiently for the civilian to explain himself.

"I insist on knowing what is transpiring here and if there is an agreement of any sort. I must protect my people here in the village and I have a right to know."

Both Gangl and Stein glared at the civilian. In war, there is little regard for civilian leadership regardless of rank.

The soldier did not reply, but Stein felt it was necessary to explain himself. "The major and I have agreed to a truce in your village. You can tell your people there will be not further fighting or destruction in Worgl from us," he said. "But remember the war is not over and others may come and destroy the peace."

"And the castle?" the Burgermeister asked.

"We have no control over what happens at Schloss Itter. Remember Herr Herring… The SS still holds the castle with its prisoners."

"I understand," Herring replied. He smiled, relieved. He tore off his Nazi armband and threw it to the ground. "I have no more need for this rag," he hissed at the two men.

All three men turned in different directions to brief their people on what Stein and Gangl had agreed.

CHAPTER 8

Kurt, awakened by a hard pounding on his door, jumped from his cot, gun in hand and ran to the door. He did not know even what time of day it was. "Who's there?" he asked, prepared to use the Luger. He did not open the door but leaned his head close. "Who's there?" he repeated.

"Kurt, it's me, Maria. I must speak with you. It's very important."

"Yes, yes, Maria," he replied, still a little groggy and disoriented from a troubled sleep. He unlocked and opened the heavy wood door. Maria rushed in and quickly closed it.

"What is it?"

"The guards keep the prisoners locked in their rooms. They ordered us not to feed them, and they watch us closely." Maria was both frightened and confused. The pattern had changed dramatically. "Oh Kurt, I'm worried. Is this it? Do they plan to shoot us?"

Kurt quickly pulled together his thoughts. "I have heard nothing. I know of no orders that were issued. Wimmer? Where is he?"

"He is with his men. They are on the grounds behind the castle."

"I will go immediately and speak with him; find out what's going on," Kurt replied. "Stay here and lock the door when I leave." He grabbed his hat and shoes, holstered his weapon.

"Kurt be careful. He is probably still angry with you."

"I will be prepared for anything, anything to protect you." He stood in the doorway.

"No Kurt, protect yourself. For me, it is too late."

"He will not harm me with the other guards around him. We do not shoot our own," he said, but he was not so confident. "And they know he is a drunk, and probably doesn't remember last night," he hoped.

Captain Wimmer and two guards returned to the main hall where Kurt greeted them. "Captain, what's the meaning of this? The prisoners must be fed."

Wimmer smiled. It was an evil smirk. "Why waste food, Captain Schrader?

Soon, today or maybe tomorrow, they will be shot."

"What do you mean? I know of no orders to execute them." He looked around at the guards present. "Lieutenant?"

The lieutenant looked down to avoid answering. Wimmer laughed. The other guards showed no emotion, nor did they express an opinion.

"You know nothing. We wait on orders from the Third SS Panzergrenadier Division, who are already close. But I may execute your traitorous whore without orders. I have not decided your fate yet, Captain, so beware."

"The Americans will arrive first, and I'll see that you are executed for this atrocity."

"You have decided your own fate, Captain," Wimmer replied sharply. "You will never see the Americans."

Kurt saw that the guards were already drinking. They talked and laughed loudly among themselves. Their voices reverberated through the cavernous room. Kurt thought they sounded like condemned men trying to bury their fears in drink. He recognized a breakdown of discipline that was moving rapidly toward chaos or worse. "Captain Wimmer, discipline your men," he ordered.

Wimmer stood and directed his attention to the three guards still talking loudly. "Attention," he called loudly. "You are the pride of Germany. Act like it. Go to your posts and do your job."

They heard him but ignored his order. They continued drinking.

Wimmer looked embarrassed. "They know the war will end soon, that they will become prisoners of either the Americans or the Russians."

Kurt drew his weapon and fired.

Everyone looked up at Captain Schrader.

"I order you to return to your posts, or I will shoot you for disobeying a direct order from a superior officer. Now! Do you hear?"

A guard, the highest-ranking enlisted man, spoke, "We are finished, Herr Captain. We are at the mercy of the enemy."

Sitting beside him, another guard spoke, "The war is over. All is lost."

"You are SS. Act like it," Kurt berated them. "If you do not return to your posts immediately, I will shoot you."

All four guards stood and saluted him to head off in different directions. "Wait," Kurt called to them. "Release the prisoners and have them fed now. I order it."

"Ja, sir," the last guard replied, and walked toward the kitchen.

Kurt and Wimmer heard yelling in the courtyard and walked quickly outside.

Maria paced about the room worried about Kurt. Suddenly she heard the gunshot. "Oh, no, Kurt. They shot him," she exclaimed, unlocked the door, and ran from the room. She reached the kitchen to see the guards disperse to their posts. "What? What has happened," she asked Bridget returning from the great hall. "Who was shot?"

Bridget smiled. "Captain Schrader ordered that the prisoners be released and fed. He fired his pistol to get their attention."

"Captain Wimmer?"

"Ha! The coward. He does nothing, only sits there drunk."

The outside guard waved to the two officers. A motorcycle with sidecar followed by a Kubelwagen had arrived. By their camouflaged uniforms, Schrader saw that it was a Waffen SS patrol. The motorcyclists dismounted, and three enlisted from the car quickly got out to join them. Two soldiers spread out around the vehicle to provide security while the other three fanned out across the castle grounds to reconnoiter the area.

A single officer—a younger lieutenant—in the woodland print camo of the Waffen SS greeted Captains Wimmer and Schrader with a stiff salute. It was returned.

"Captain Wimmer?" the lieutenant asked, looking at both men. "I am Captain Wimmer."

"We are from the 3rd Battalion commanded by Major Joaquin Speers and have come to assess your defenses. The main force is approximately fifteen miles east and is in movement. They plan to arrive here tomorrow. You must prepare your defenses to make a stand against the Americans in our final battle for the Third Reich. We shall make it a glorious one. Heil Hitler!" All gave the straight-arm salute, even though both Wimmer and Schrader knew Hitler was dead.

"We are ordered to guard the VIP prisoners only, not battle the Americans. Our command in Dachau ordered it.," Wimmer said.

"Your orders have changed. You will join us by order of Major Speers." He handed Wimmer the written order, which he took and began to examine. Wimmer was very careful not to allow Schrader to read it.

"What about our prisoners?" Kurt asked.

"They are high-ranking French prisoners. Is that not correct?" "That is correct, Lieutenant," Wimmer replied.

"They are no longer of use to us and will certainly create problems when we fight the Americans. We are few and we cannot allocate men to guard them."

"What are you suggesting, Lieutenant?" Kurt asked.

"By order of Major Speers, we are to execute them. Dig a deep ditch in the woods well behind the castle," he said. "When the battalion arrives, we will complete the task. Is that understood?"

"I understand," Wimmer replied. He looked worried. "Do you know the size of the American force and if they have close-in fighter support?"

"Are you worried, Captain?"

"No, no, but the war will soon end. Is all this necessary?"

"If Major Speers, by order of Himmler, says it is, then, Captain, it is necessary."

Kurt watched Wimmer. He seemed concerned about the order, but he suspected, Wimmer was more worried about his own skin. He easily saw the anxiety written on his face.

"We have heard the Americans are already nearing Innsbruck. Their armor could arrive any day. Do their tanks not outnumber yours, Lieutenant?" Kurt asked.

The much younger lieutenant looked hard but only at Wimmer. "We fight for our honor, and don't expect to survive. Have you lost your courage, Captain? Are you not in command here?"

"I am," Wimmer said, not overly confident.

"Has your easy duty here while we have been fighting the Russians softened you?"

Kurt listened to the exchange and realized quickly that if the SS tried to hold the castle against the much larger American force, no one could expect to survive. He agreed with the lieutenant on that one thing.

"We will prepare for your arrival, Lieutenant," Wimmer said, not altogether convincing.

The lieutenant waved to his men, and then walked to his vehicle. They loaded up, started their vehicles and left.

Kurt looked at Wimmer and smiled. "Captain, I don't think either of us will survive."

"Don't be so certain, Captain," Wimmer replied. They returned to the main hall.

Later, the prisoners, surrounded by their guards, sat around the large table. Captain Wimmer entered and marched to the head of the table. "Enjoy your meal. There will be no more for you. When the SS battalion arrives, you will be shot." He smiled, turned, and walked toward the castle ramparts. Two guards followed him.

His words scared the hell out of the prisoners, but he bluntly told them what they already knew. Each felt their impending death with a renewed sense of dread. They talked among themselves. Edouard Daladier, former premier of France, stood to speak. "Captain, wait."

Wimmer turned to face the table.

"I must protest. What you are planning to do is in complete disregard of the Geneva Convention, and all rules of civilized society. The war will end soon enough. Why not allow us to leave?"

Marie Cailliau stood to support Daladier. "You cannot get away with this atrocity. You sir are a war criminal, and my brother will hunt you down."

Borotra stood to plead his own case. "I have done nothing to warrant such extreme cruelty. I demand that you allow me to leave."

Everyone looked at him with contempt and disdain.

Maria and Bridget stood in the far side of the room silent but listening closely.

Wimmer, seeing Maria, smiled. "Lieutenant, take the traitor and lock her in the dungeon."

The lieutenant looked at him. "Sir?"

"Take her downstairs, and then disarm Captain Schrader. That's an order. Take two men." He again smiled. "Did you think I had forgotten, Schrader? I am still commandant here."

"Captain?" a younger guard asked.

"You heard me. Do it now." Wimmer then turned to leave the hall. He staggered up the stairs to his room. Inside, he flopped down in his chair and reached for the bottle of Schnapps—his last.

"I should have him shot for treason now," he mumbled to no one. "Will the men obey? I wonder." He considered his options. Even drunk he knew he had few, and none were good. The Panzers could arrive tomorrow, or most certainly the following day. I will have them do it. Yes, that's it. A firing squad and I'll have them shoot the woman, too. They will all be shot anyway. But the Americans will arrive with their endless tanks and fighter planes. They're fools, he thought. The SS… Their commander is not a reasonable man to continue fighting. Everyone will be killed, or worse, captured and executed. What does any of it accomplish with the war ending any day?

Automatic and small arms fire opened up as the motorcycle with its two riders passed them. The shooting was from the trees nearest the road. The two riders were both hit, and the motorcycle spun out of control, coming to rest against a pine. The driver lay lifeless on the road, bleeding from his head and shoulder. The other in the passenger seat struggled to escape while small arms fire continued to zip overhead.

The lone soldier finally freed himself from the cycle and scrambled for cover in the ditch and woods.

"Get them! Get them!" he heard in German above the gunfire. "Before the others get here."

The Kubelwagen with its passengers easily heard the shooting. The car slid to a halt and all four bailed out. More than fifty meters behind the ambush site, they quickly organized a response.

"Fan out," the lieutenant ordered. "Try to get behind them." Two men silently moved into the pine forest while the lieutenant and his driver remained on the road firing their pistols at the ambushers. Finding targets was difficult for the soldiers as the ambushers moved through the forest silently and quickly, but the ambushers were unaware two soldiers circled around behind them.

The soldier from the sidecar began to return fire. A heated exchange ensued with neither side giving an inch.

Suddenly, the soldiers in the woods opened up. The ambushers were caught in a crossfire.

"Let's go!" the lieutenant ordered from behind their vehicle, and both men advanced down the road toward the motorcycle. They fired relentlessly at the attackers but had to stop to reload before reaching their two comrades along the road.

The fighting quickly changed as the two soldiers caught the attackers in a vice. Their ranks evaporated, and lacking discipline, the remaining partisans, fearful of being trapped and killed, had to flee with their comrades deeper into the woods.

The lieutenant and his driver neared the motorcycle with its riders. They poured every round they had into the trees. The firing from the woods dissolved into sporadic sniping and then abruptly stopped. The lieutenant rushed to the wounded man in the bushes. "Are you hit?" he asked him.

"Ja, but only slightly."

The lieutenant then moved to the man lying lifeless on the road. Turning him over, he checked his vitals, looked at the wounds.

"Is he…?" another soldier asked. "Ja," the lieutenant replied.

The two soldiers emerged from the woods, neither wounded. Seeing their comrade lying prone on the road, they ran to him. "Is he dead?" one asked.

"Ja," the lieutenant replied again. He stood to survey the scene. "Partisans?" "Ja," the soldier replied. "Five, maybe six. We killed two and the rest ran." "What kind of weapons?"

"American, some British, and one of the dead had an automatic rifle beside him. One of our weapons."

"Deserters—traitors I suspect—are with them," the lieutenant replied, concerned about the growing threat from the resistance. "They are everywhere in these woods. I think they hide among the refugees. I must warn Majors Speers," he said. "Bring the car and we'll return to the battalion."

CHAPTER 9

The lieutenant and his recon patrol, with one wounded, one dead man, and minus the motorcycle, found the main force moving in their direction only a few miles from them. They navigated their way between tanks and refugees clinging to the road. Finally, they reached Major Speers, who had halted his vehicle to wait for their arrival.

The lieutenant without hesitation sought out his major. The others removed their casualties from the Kubelwagen and carried them back.

"Major," he said, out of breath, "I met with Captain Wimmer, surveyed the grounds, and gave him your order. The captain will prepare for our arrival." He had to speak loudly over engine noise. "But the man cannot be trusted."

Speers took his time, refusing to be hurried by the vehicles passing around them. "What of their defenses? Can the castle sustain an attack by artillery and from the air?" He had already suspected Captain Wimmer of lacking the martial spirit. A garrison soldier who lacks proper motivation, Speers thought.

"The castle is built of heavy stone, and I think able to withstand heavy fire. The walls and ramparts offer good fields of fire. A moat surrounds it, with a single entrance by a stone bridge. If we have a good day, we could prepare to give the Americans a good fight. Our greatest problem could be lack of food and ammo to hold out against superior forces. The current inhabitants have little food, and the guards have only light weapons with limited ammo," the lieutenant reported.

Major Speers listened quietly without interrupting the lieutenant's briefing. "Captain Wimmer's prisoners?" he asked when the lieutenant finished. "The French diplomats?"

"They must be dealt with, sir."

"Yes, of course. How many are there?"

"At least twenty, plus servants from Dachau, and they are about to run out of rations."

"A liability we cannot accept," Speers said. "Where do you think the Americans are now?"

"Their advance elements are near Innsbruck, but they have slowed."

Speers smiled, hearing the first bit of good news. "Good, good, Lieutenant. We have an opportunity to beat them to the castle. Then we can give them a nice surprise."

"Yes, sir."

"What happened to your team?"

"We were ambushed several kilometers outside the village of Worgl." "By whom?"

"Austrian resistance. Partisans in the forest, but we were able to drive them off. We killed two and the remainder fled into the woods. Sir, the area is also filled with deserters who assist the partisans. We know this. They are emboldened with the Americans so close."

"We lost one man killed. Any wounded?"

"Sergeant Goff, a grazing wound in his arm. He should be back at full duty shortly."

"Lieutenant, you and your men have performed well." They saluted.

"One more thing. Spread the word: all deserters will be summarily shot as traitors to the Fatherland."

A Panzer Tiger rumbled slowly by them. Men on top steadily held their gaze forward, looking toward the next battle. Each hoped it would be their last.

"Sir, I have a question."

Major Speers turned back to the junior officer. "Yes?" "What of the Russians. Will they attack our rear?"

"I think not. They have Vienna and know the Americans are very close. I think it will take them a few days to consolidate the city, and for their supply lines to catch up."

The lieutenant returned to his vehicle while Major Speers mounted his. They moved out, heading west.

While Major Speers' armored force steadily approached Castle Itter, Major Gangl's surviving Wehrmacht soldiers set up camp in the village square of Worgl. The SS Battalion's plans were unknown to them as they had, days earlier, lost radio contact with other elements of the German Army, and Major Speers knew nothing of Gangl and his small contingent of Wehrmacht soldiers.

The partisans came and went. There was little coordination and no talk between the two opposing groups, but there was no trouble either.

Major Gangl searched the village looking for a working radio. He desperately wanted to hear the latest news. Had the war ended? He had to know.

Walking along an unusually quiet street, he pulled a worn photo from his gray tunic—a picture of a young woman. He touched it gently, as he had a thousand times during the past months. "Soon, soon I pray the war will end and we can be together," he whispered to himself.

Sergeant Krouse ran up to him and saluted. That seemed an unusual action for his ranking NCO in a combat situation.

Saluting under fire gets soldiers killed and everyone, especially an NCO, knows this. It must be important, Major Gangl thought. "Sergeant, what is it?" he asked, seeing how excited Krouse acted.

"Major, we have received news of the war," Sergeant Krouse blurted out. "Let's hear it," he replied, surprised.

"Sir, the war continues. Germany has not yet surrendered. The enemy pushes in from all sides. The Russians have destroyed Berlin, and the capitol is on fire. We are fighting the Red Army in the streets of the city. I fear all is lost," Sergeant Krouse reported with barely contained emotion.

Gangl stopped to consider the news. Should I feel sorrow or relief? he asked himself.

"The men, sir… They are ready to go home. It is time, I think."

"I understand. Everyone wants to go home." Gangl listened without interrupting. "Still, we must stay together," he finally said. "You have heard the planes and the artillery in the distance. The war surrounds us, and we have no place to run."

"Is this village safe for us with the partisans here? I think we must remain vigilant, or they will turn on us."

"Yes, Sergeant. Tell the men."

CHAPTER 10

Two SS guards watched, rifles slung, as prisoners, Generals Gamelin and Weygand, dug a deep trench in the woods behind the castle. Wimmer had earlier chosen the generals for the odious task. It was his way of humiliating his former adversaries.

"Why must we do this, Heinz? When the Americans come, they will shoot us," the thin bald guard asked. The others called him Harry to mock him.

"Ja, that is probably true, but we have our orders. You heard Captain Schrader. He will also shoot us if we disobey," Heinz replied. One of them leaned against a tree while the other sat on a nearby tree stump. Watching the two older and defeated Frenchmen dig provided a certain amount of entertainment for them. "Why did you stop, Herr General?" Heinz asked with considerable sarcasm.

The general said nothing. He wiped perspiration from his brow with the back of a sleeved arm, and then resumed digging.

"Deeper, deeper. There are many of you," the other guard said. "We will get the women to take the dirt away."

Heinz laughed.

"We have been very lucky. They could have sent us to Russia." "Lucky to be Schutzstaffel and prison guards."

"But this is no good, no good at all. Now we must take care of ourselves. It is too late for the Third Reich," Heinz said, concerned. "I have children, a wife."

"I also have children," the guard replied. "We must have a plan of escape before the Americans get here."

They looked at the diggers. "Dig! It must be done today."

"Take me with you then," Heinz replied. "The time is right. If we wait one more day, it will be too late. The Americans come from the west and south. The Russians come from the east."

"The time is tonight, I fear."

"But where does that leave for us to escape?"

"We will go deep into the mountains and wait."

The two French generals looked at each other. Growing tired, the older men continued to dig. They knew they were digging their own grave. "This is absurd. I cannot do this any longer," General Weygand growled. "Hey you," he called to the guards. "Shoot me now. I am finished with this nonsense."

The guards paused, not knowing quite how to respond. Heinz stood to walk over to the two generals. He spit in the hole. "Good enough. Now return to your quarters."

The two Frenchmen left. Heinz shrugged. "Not our problem, is it?" His comrade shrugged.

Captain Wimmer watched from the above ramparts. Like the guards, Wimmer also worried about his survival. He sighed loudly and turned to stagger back inside. He was drinking. "Lieutenant, Lieutenant, where the hell are you?"

"Here sir," Lieutenant Klinz replied. He rounded the corner behind Wimmer. Wimmer stopped and leaned against the stone. "Have you placed a guard on

Captain Schrader?"

"Sir?"

"We must watch him closely. When they arrive, I will turn him over as a traitor."

"No need, sir," Klinz replied. "The captain does nothing but worry over the woman traitor. He will never leave without her."

"Yes, yes, quite so. No problem with him—the fool."

Maria leaned against the damp stone wall of the medieval dungeon, considering her fate. At least, he didn't have me shot, she thought. She walked to the narrow, barred window in the heavy wood door to try to look out. She glimpsed a ray of light from somewhere above, but only a passing glimmer. No light anywhere in the cell. The almost total darkness disoriented her as she felt for the walls and any furniture. There was none.

She could only listen for footsteps outside the heavy door. But she knew the next time she saw a guard it may well be to execute her. Was that better than spending days in a dark hole without food or water? She wondered.

She quit pacing an hour ago. A useless waste of energy, she decided, and sat on the cold, damp stone floor which allowed her plenty of time to focus, not unlike in the packed railcar on the way to Dachau. Her impending death was still by firing squad at the hands of the SS, but she had to force that from her thoughts. I'm not afraid any longer. Maria was too angry to be afraid.

Captain Wimmer, she thought, now he's one despicable character. A drunk and a rapist. She shuddered when she thought of him touching her. What kind of mother had brought him into the world? Maria shook her head. Nothing more than a gutter rat like the rest of them, she easily concluded.

But Kurt? Thinking of him saddened her. He had a good family and a proper education, I know that, yet he is part of that scum, no better than Wimmer. Once, she had a brother with whom she could share her hopes and dreams. Seeing him now in the horrid black uniform with the runes on the collar disgusted her. What evil he's done since I last saw him.

His father was right about him, she sadly remembered. Kurt was a weak man, a follower. He didn't even have the courage to defend my honor, the honor of an Austrian woman. Maria believed the other guards would have supported him if he had taken command. But in her hour of need, he failed. He failed at his one opportunity to show courage and bring honor to himself. Does Hitler's evil hold him in his spell?

But he did save me from the horrid beast. He protected me. That must show he is not like the rest of them. I must not forget that, she thought. She sighed deeply in the darkness with its smells, reminding her of the train to Dachau.

Josef, my Josef. She dreamed of his touch. She felt her breasts where the beast Wimmer had touched her. She shook at the thought of the man's hands all over her body.

Josef never wanted to go to war, not like the others. He was an engineer not a soldier. He wanted to build things not destroy them. She remembered how Rolf urged them to escape to London or New York when the war began. He offered to pay our all of our living expenses, but Josef refused. He said that was dishonorable. His country was at war and the only honorable choice was to serve.

But to fight in a crazy man's war against the civilized world? Honor has nothing to do with that. Honor is defending your family, not killing Russians or Englishmen. I will never understand men, she thought.

Maria sighed deeply and tried to sleep, but sleep was impossible. She could think of nothing but her childhood brothers. With Kurt here and ready to die beside her, she knew she had to overlook his stupidity, but he still disgusted her. A Nazi.

When the guard threw her in the cell, she noticed that the old lock no longer secured the door. He braced it with a sturdy timber he found lying along the wall.

Maria had an idea. She stepped back against the far wall and ran to throw her shoulder at the door. She repeated those efforts until her shoulders ached from the pounding. Soon bruises covered both shoulders.

She shook the door with both hands on the bars and sensed that something had changed. I'll try again, she decided. Twice more she assaulted the door, and finally she heard a noise from outside. She checked the door. It was loose and unlatched. The timber had dislodged and fallen to the stone floor.

The old wood door swung open. Maria was free.

Wimmer slowly staggered back to his room. He started the day much as he had ended the last. He decided it was time for another drink. He walked through the hall toward his room. He felt everyone's eyes on him, most importantly, Schrader's.

Kurt, disarmed and a prisoner like the others, watched him with contempt. "General, soon it will end," Kurt said to Weygand, who had just returned from his odious task.

"Not soon enough," the general replied.

Wimmer suddenly stopped before he left the hall. He turned and smiled, as only a drunk can.

Kurt turned to the commandant. "You will hang for this. It does not matter if I die, the Americans will find you out. They will hang you for committing mass murder."

"Shut up traitor," Wimmer replied. "Shoot him if he moves from the hall. He is allowed to go to only two places—here and his room."

"Ja," the guard said. He frowned but did as ordered. "What about the privy, Captain?" Kurt asked.

"Put the request in writing," Wimmer said and disappeared from the hall—to everyone's relief.

Kurt spent the remainder of the day and evening conversing with the prisoners. Food was scarce, but wine was plentiful. By order of Wimmer, they could drink as much as they wanted. "A final treat," he told them.

Feeling the effect of the wine, Kurt returned slowly to his room followed by the guard. "Beware of the captain, Private, or he will get you killed. If I were you, I would leave this place quickly before the Americans arrive," Kurt told him.

The young private listened quietly but said nothing. Kurt entered the room and locked the door.

Early the next morning, a hard pounding on the door awakened him. "Who?" he asked, reaching for his weapon.

"Captain, Captain, wake up. Please wake up."

"Who is it?" Kurt asked.

"Bridget," the young woman replied.

Kurt unlocked it, and the door swung open. The young woman stood there, a look of confusion on her face.

"What time is it?" he asked.

"Morning," she said. "Something is happening that I don't understand. The guards, they have... I have searched," Bridget said, unable to contain her anxiety.

"What has happened? Captain Wimmer?" he asked. He dressed quickly and followed Bridget.

"They are all gone. We looked everywhere in the castle. Captain Wimmer, the sergeant, all the other soldiers are gone. We prepared the last of the food rations and took them to the hall, but the guards had locked the doors to their rooms."

"Strange, very strange," Kurt said, trying to understand. "We must find a way to free everyone. The keys could be in the castle, perhaps, in Wimmer's room. Let's look." They rushed up the stairs to the commandant's room and knocked. No answer. They tried the door. It was unlocked, swinging open with a slight push. They entered cautiously and began to search the room.

"Where could he have gone, Herr Captain?" Bridget asked. She did not move from her spot near the door, fearful he could return at any time.

"I don't understand," Kurt replied. He rummaged through the room, looking for anything to tell them what happened. He found the ring of keys in a drawer and held them up. "You will take these and unlock the doors. Go!"

"Ja, Herr Captain," she replied. "But what has happened to them?"

"They have run away. Neither surrendering nor fighting, the cowards have chosen to flee," Kurt told her. "Now go quickly." He continued to rummage through the room. In the lower right desk drawer, he saw a folded document, and thinking it important, reached in to retrieve it. Seeing it was the order from the SS Battalion commander, Kurt sat in Wimmer's chair and began to read. The order confirmed all that Wimmer had been saying about the imminent arrival of the Panzers, but what caught his immediate attention was the order to execute all the prisoners. He had even designated men to do the task.

Maria ran into the room. "Kurt, what is happening?" Kurt looked up. "Maria, you've escaped… How?"

"The lock was broken so I forced my way out. I ran into Bridget and she told me," Maria said, excited. "Are we free of them?"

"The Panzers are coming, probably tomorrow. We cannot allow them to take Schloss Itter. That would mean certain death for all of us." He handed her the order.

"The Americans will come."

"The Americans? Who knows where they are, and it could take them two or three days to reach us."

"What are we to do?"

"I don't know yet, but we must come up with a plan. Get everyone together." "Can't we run away from here before the SS come?"

"Where, Maria, where?" he replied. "It is too dangerous, and many would probably be captured and killed. Remember, they are old and not very strong, and they are French who do not know these woods. We must fight and try to hold them off until the Americans arrive. That is our only option to survive."

She looked at him, frowning.

"Maria, I cannot stop you if you want to flee this place. You are young and strong, and Austrian. You could find the partisans."

Maria was not convinced of his strategy, but she trusted him. "I will stay and fight the bastards," she said, feeling suddenly empowered. I have faced torture, rape, and death by shooting," she said. "Now, it is time to take a stand. They can do no more than shoot me, and I will have died honorably."

He smiled upon hearing her say that, appreciating her support. He felt the strength in her words. "Let's go. We must get everyone and plan a defense." They ran from the room.

CHAPTER 11

May 4, 1945, 0600 hrs.

Everyone gathered in the great hall of the castle. Most of the VIPs sat at the large table while the servants and Schrader stood behind them. A look of confusion shadowed each face—all but Kurt, Maria, and Bridget. Kurt moved to the head of the table and prepared to speak. The large room grew quiet with everyone looking to the SS officer.

"Please listen to me. What I have to say is very important and concerns the survival of each of us."

The VIPs greeted his initial statement with more confusion. Most had a look of "What does this SS officer, our prison guard, want from us?"

"Please, we have much to discuss, or all is lost. Trust what I tell you," he continued.

Maria Cailliau could take no more of the mystery foisted on them by their captor. "How can we trust what you say? You are SS—our captor—like the others. You have orders to shoot us."

"No, I am different. Captain Wimmer and his guards fled during the night. I don't know when." He allowed that to sink in before continuing. "I am with you and have as much to lose when the SS troops come as you. You must believe that."

He looked around and saw mostly skeptical and disbelieving faces.

Maria, seeing their reaction, stepped forward. "I know him. He is not a killer like the others. He is an honorable man who wishes to help us escape from the horror." She was not convinced but knew Kurt could help them survive. Somehow.

He looked to Maria and smiled, appreciating her critical support. "And you have no choice but to listen to what I have to say. When you have heard me out, you can decide your own destiny."

The VIP prisoners and the servants tried to grasp what had transpired, but General Weygand understood immediately what was happening. "Then we are free? You will not stop us from leaving this place?"

The hall erupted in cheering, transformed as if by magic. Suddenly, there was hope on everyone's face. A dark, cloudy morning with everyone awoken to the prospect of dying had changed within seconds to one of great joy. Even the servants, having come from the camps felt it in their hearts.

"Wait… Please. The war has not ended. A battalion of Waffen SS troops with tanks is a short distance from here. They are ordered to take the castle and fight the Americans. And to shoot us… Yes, even me."

"Then we must escape before it's too late," General Weygand replied,

"I think a celebration is in order," the former tennis champ, Borotra, exclaimed.

"Yes, break out the champagne," Alfred Cailliau said happily.

The others looked at the man and smiled. "Do you think we have champagne here, Alfred?" his wife asked with a gentle smile, her first in several years.

"Wait, hear what I have to tell you," Kurt broke in. "The SS is too close, and the forests are deep and hidden within are partisans and deserters. They could easily shoot you before they know who you are."

"What of the roads going west and north toward the Americans?" Paul Reynaud asked. "If we could reach the Allies in the west, we would be safe."

"That is true, but we do not know how far from here they are, and the roads everywhere are dangerous, and we have the older ones and the women to think of. If the Americans have reached Innsbruck, that is 38 miles from here. Too far to walk without food and even water to drink."

General Henri Giraud rose to speak. "Do we have weapons?"

"We will search the castle for weapons," Michael Clemenceau said. "Jean, come with me." Both men stood and hurriedly left the room.

"We don't have many choices. A run for it towards Innsbruck is the best plan. Some may not make it, but most could. That is better than our odds of surviving if we stay," Madame Cailliau replied from her chair.

"Far too risky. There is already fighting in the woods around us. We hear it. I think taking a stand here and holding out for the Americans is our best plan," Kurt argued. "Here we have thick walls to protect us." He knew he could leave the castle at any time and allow them to fend for themselves, but Maria would never leave them. He could not leave her.

"Then I will pray the Americans arrive before the SS," Madam Cailliau said, reluctantly giving in to Schrader. She was the oldest and sickliest. She knew she could not survive in the woods more than a day or two.

"Time is rapidly running out. We must prepare now," Kurt said. "We must reach the forward elements of the American armies and plead our case for immediate rescue."

The others had stopped talking among themselves and were giving Captain Schrader full attention. "We need a volunteer to attempt to reach the Americans. He must go perhaps ten miles or thirty. We simply do not know."

Andre Cuckovic, camp inmate and castle handy man, stepped forward from behind the table. "I will go. I saw a bicycle with good tires in an outbuilding. I will take it and make better time."

"Go now. It is, I believe, our best option," Kurt said.

He's trying to remain positive, Maria thought, watching.

Andre appeared very excited about his mission. "I was supposed to die in the camps like my father, mother, and wife, so I have nothing to lose." He ran from the room to prepare for his mission.

The two men returned from their weapons search and rushed forward to speak with Kurt. "Captain, we found a body—Sergeant Otto. He was in his room, the door locked, so we broke it down. Suicide, bullet to the head."

Kurt was unmoved. "Did you get his weapon?"

"Yes, he had several and ammunition," Alfred replied.

"Place him in the ditch dug yesterday and bury him. Leave his information so that he can be identified later."

Alfred and two others left to assist with the dead man.

"The Germans have tanks. How do we defend against them," General Weygand asked.

Clemenceau with Jean Borotra returned to the hall, their arms filled with weapons. They laid them out on the table. Kurt examined them. "I see two rifles, an automatic, and the rest are pistols. Do we have ammunition for each?"

"Yes, but it must be collected," Clemenceau replied. "There may be additional weapons. We haven't looked everywhere."

"Good," Kurt said. "We will have to fight with these, stall them, and try to hold on until we are rescued."

"And if the Americans are too late to save us?" Weygand asked.

Kurt shrugged. "We will have done all that we could, fought valiantly, and given our all. What more?"

Some at the table still looked upon Captain Schrader suspiciously, but everyone understood they had few options available to them. Kurt went from prisoner to prisoner, and from servant to servant soliciting approval for his plan. That was difficult as he was used to giving orders without questioning. Democracy was a new concept for him. Each except Madame Cailliau nodded their head, acquiescing, even though most harbored grave misgivings.

"Your plan concerns me greatly. Are you our former captor and now our savior? How can this be?" Marie Cailliau said, again voicing her concerns. "Perhaps, it would be better to hide in the woods."

The old woman is determined to force her will on the others, Maria thought.

"Hide in the woods? How will you eat, drink? You do not even speak German. If the SS capture you, they will shoot you like a deserter. If you hide, you would be dead in a matter of days, foolish woman," General Weygand said.

Kurt tried to ignore the bickering. "I know there are partisans in the village of Worgl. We must contact them and beg for their assistance. Who will volunteer to go?"

The hall was quiet as each looked to the other. Kurt waited patiently for a response but received none. Predictable, he thought. "I will go then. Under a flag of truce."

"That is wise, I think. He obviously speaks their language, and hopefully, they will honor a flag of truce," General Weygand observed, reluctantly giving in to the plan.

"Can we trust that you won't run away, abandon us. You are SS like the others," Francois De La Rocque said, breaking his silence.

"You have no choice but to trust me," Kurt replied evenly. "I give you the word of an officer in the German army."

La Rocque did not reply.

"I will go then," Maria said. "They won't shoot a woman under a flag of truce... I hope."

"No Maria, it is my duty. General Weygand, you are in charge until I return." Weygand nodded his acceptance.

Paul Reynaud stood, agitated. Kurt looked and nodded to the former premier of France for him to speak.

"I must object. I fought the German invasion while General Weygand tried to flee. I should command here until you return."

The others nodded their heads in agreement. Kurt saw their near unanimous approval for Reynaud. "If all agree, Premier Reynaud will assume responsibility." All but the general and the fascists agreed.

"The SS will crush you, and you will all die anyway. Fools. Surrender now and appeal to them. Beg for mercy," La Rocque said, his voice laced with contempt.

"Do you, Monsieur Fascist, think they will spare you?" Marie Cailliau asked.

La Rocque did not reply. Poncet and Marcel entered the hall again with several additional Mausers and boxes of ammo they had uncovered. "We found more ammo but could not carry it."

"Excellent," Kurt said. "I go now to Worgl. Monsieur Reynaud, prepare the defenses."

Everyone watched him leave.

Kurt found a large white handkerchief and began to tie it to his cane when Maria rushed into the room. "Please be careful. When they see the uniform you wear, they may want to shoot you," she said concerned. "We do not know who controls the village."

He looked at her and then nodded he understood. "We've created too many enemies and no friends. I hope their sense of honor allows me at least the opportunity to talk with them. It is not too much to ask, even of an SS officer."

Maria hugged him. "Please be careful. They will kill what they fear the most." She kissed him on the cheek and watched him leave.

Kurt and Paul Reynaud stood together in the courtyard looking out at the only gate and across the narrow bridge. "They can come only from that way and must cross that bridge. There is no other way to get inside the castle. That's where we must stop them."

"I agree, Captain," Reynaud replied and turned to shake Kurt's hand. "Good luck."

"Thank you, Prime Minister for trusting me with this mission. I will not let you down. But, if you do not see me by evening, know that I have been killed or captured. Good luck to you." Kurt began to walk toward the gate. He then stopped suddenly and returned to Reynaud.

He removed a chain and locket from around his neck. "Please take this and give it to Maria." He handed Reynaud the locket and chain. "She'll know what it is."

Seeing a family heirloom and sensing its value, Reynaud took the locket and smiled. "I will certainly, Captain." He saluted Kurt. "We place our lives in your hands."

"Thank you," he replied. "I will not fail." He turned, walked down the gravel lane and out over the bridge toward Worgl, six miles away.

From an upper window of the castle, Maria watched him depart. She wiped away a tear, not knowing if she would ever see him again. "This terrible war," she said under her breath. "So many are gone, and for what?" She walked down the steps to return to the great hall.

Reynaud greeted her. "The captain gave me this to give to you. He said you would know what it is."

Maria took it and smiled. She recognized it immediately. Opening it, she showed small photographs of two very young faces to Reynaud. "Here is my husband, Josef." She touched it. "And the other is of Kurt when they were boys. I think it was Kurt's most cherished possession, having carried it through the war." A single tear graced her cheek. "We felt differently about Hitler and the war, but he was still my brother. Now he is gone, too."

Captain Wimmer and the five guards left the castle well before light. Wimmer had made his decision and invited the others to join him. They agreed. "We are better in numbers," he told them. They left their positions at the castle lightly armed with pistols and carrying only the ammo on their cartridge belts. He had pounded on Otto's door with no response. They could not wait any longer.

The small group soon discovered that they had little knowledge of the terrain, since all six were from Germany, and had traveled little outside the immediate area. After a short discussion a mile outside the gate, they agreed to travel south.

Nearing the village of Worgl as the sun graced the sky, they came under fire — ambushed. The battle was quick. Firing from behind trees, the ambushers fired off their weapons and fled, but they caught the six openly walking down the road, and they became easy prey dressed in their black uniforms. Having no combat experience, the men provided little resistance and fled quickly each running in a different direction.

Before Wimmer was able to collect his men, and find sanctuary in the woods, they had lost two of their number, one man shot dead on the road while the other tried to flee into the bushes. Fighting the partisans had expended much of their ammo.

Now knowing the area was alive with partisans, deserters and the SS somewhere, they decided to stay off the road and began to travel cautiously through the woods. Wimmer placed one man way out front as a point.

Seeing armed men among the trees, the point man returned excited to inform the others.

"Partisans," Wimmer told the others. "They're everywhere. We must go a different way." They had to change course, mostly traveling in the woods and on trails, hoping to avoid another ambush. Wimmer had studied maps of the area before he departed and had memorized the roads to safety. But in the woods, disoriented and confused, they did not know where they actually were.

The captain, the others saw, was drinking heavily. Each knew that did not improve their chances of finding a safe haven. Irritated, they grew even more concerned when Wimmer began stumbling. He fell on his face several times and had to be assisted.

"Captain, you must keep your wits about you," Heinz told him after picking him up, and helping him navigate the brush and bushes. "We have a long way before Switzerland."

"Switzerland, ha," Wimmer replied.

The others looked at him surprised, but before they discovered what he meant, they heard loud talking from the road that they paralleled, and soon encountered increasing numbers of refugees, many in the woods.

They tried to engage them for assistance and intelligence, but realized their black uniforms were easily recognizable, and drawing their attention.

Everyone in Europe it seemed had come to know what the black uniforms with the lighting runes meant.

"We have to get out of these," Heinz said. "Find someone your size and take his clothes." With stragglers and outliers everywhere, they quickly found new clothes. Each isolated a victim and through barter, intimidation, or physical threats found at least a shirt to change into. They then buried the black uniforms.

"What unit is this, Captain?" Heinz asked, seeing a Kubelwagen parked along the road. They saw four SS soldiers standing nearby.

"Shut up and stay down," Wimmer ordered. "It's the SS Battalion moving toward the castle. They cannot see us or we're dead dressed like this."

Now three, they slid into a ravine to hide. The soldiers did not move from their spot on the road. Waiting, the day rapidly began to slip away for Wimmer and his men.

Each knew they could not hide there for long. Wimmer knew the soldiers were the advance of the main element of the Panzers who would soon be upon them. He estimated they were only about seven kilometers from the castle and feared the battalion would prepare for any attack on Itter from this location.

"We must move further into the forest," he whispered. He looked at his two companions and saw fear.

"No, too dangerous," Heinz replied. "They will see us." He seemed frozen to the ground. Lieutenant Klinz also refused to move, knowing that wearing civilian clothes, they would be called deserters, which they were.

CHAPTER 12

Walking the best he could with his bad leg, Captain Schrader neared Worgl carefully. Luckily, he encountered no one on the road. From a hill overlooking the village, he was able to reconnoiter the main streets. He saw Wehrmacht soldiers, not SS in their camo, several without weapons, and others with weapons moving about mixed with villagers. That could be a good sign, he hoped, better than finding partisans who would rather shoot first at a soldier then ask questions.

He examined his flag of truce, took a deep breath, and then marched slowly into town. He was unarmed and hatless, and not wearing the black uniform of the SS prison guards, but the camouflage of a Panzer soldier. He hoped that would discourage trigger-happy and untrained partisans. Hearing rustling in the bushes just outside the main street, he touched his empty holster. It was a nervous reflex action. Nothing but a squirrel. Passing the first house, he began to wave the white handkerchief tied to his cane high over his head.

Walking down the first cobblestone street still waving the handkerchief, he encountered no one, not even a dog or cat. The streets were suddenly deserted, but he felt hundreds of eyes following him. That's how five years of war touches you, he thought, knowing their fear.

Suddenly, from both sides of the street, armed men appeared. From one side, they were dressed as civilians, but on the other, they were clearly German soldiers. Both groups watched him closely. How strange, he thought, armed enemies coexisting on the same street. He decided to approach one of the German soldiers.

"Where is your commander?" he asked. "I must speak with your commanding officer." He quickly scanned the man's uniform to determine what unit he served.

The soldier, at first, did not answer him, only glared at his uniform with the lighting runes. "SS butcherers. What do you want here?" He saw Schrader was unarmed.

"I must speak with your commander," Kurt said, urgency in his voice. Another soldier arrived to support the first. The partisans watched the exchange, which to them, appeared to be discussion between German soldiers, but they kept their distance.

"We should shoot you where you stand," the first soldier said.

Major Gangl stepped from the doorway to observe. "What's going on?" he asked Sergeant Krouse.

"I don't know, but I see the intruder is SS," Krouse replied.

"Send him to me," Josef said, calling to the two soldiers. He saw the white handkerchief.

"Let's go," the first soldier said. He grabbed Kurt's arm. "One of Hitler's own. We should shoot him," he said to the other. The common soldiers had come to hate the SS, mostly for well-publicized war crimes that civilians often blamed on them. They escorted him the short distance to Gangl, passing a water fountain in the center of the village. "Herr Major, he is SS and asks to speak with you. He has a flag of truce." At that, both soldiers smiled, thinking it ironic.

"A major commands you? Then you are a battalion strong," Kurt said. He was hopeful he had found the support he needed.

"Ask the major," the soldier said with contempt. They reached the doorstep and Major Gangl.

"Where did he come from?" Josef asked, confused. "He came down the road from the old castle."

"From Schloss Itter? The SS prison the partisans speak of?" Now standing only a few feet apart, Josef looked more closely at the man's face. He recognized him.

"He came alone, sir, and not armed."

"Join me," he said to Captain Schrader, and allowed him entrance into his command post. Both men stared at the other. Neither could believe his eyes.

"Kurt, is it really you?" Josef asked, shocked. "Josef?"

They embraced. Josef became tearful. "So many years, I cannot believe this. A miracle that you are alive," Josef said, overwhelmed with surprise. "But what happened to you? I saw you limp."

"Only a cheap Russian bullet, but almost healed."

"I heard you were killed in the Ukraine," Josef said, still looking at Kurt's leg. "A miracle, truly."

Kurt smiled broadly and reached up to ruffle his stepbrother's hair. "We thought you were dead… in France."

Sergeant Krause listened to the two men. Their warmth toward each other perplexed him.

"Josef, I have good news. Maria is at Schloss Itter. I found her at Dachau and rescued her."

"Dachau? I don't believe it. How? She was safe on your father's estate. What happened?" He was overwhelmed. "I must go to her immediately."

"That is a story she must tell."

"Then we must go. I have a vehicle," he repeated, excited.

"Wait, Josef. She is safe for the moment with French prisoners. The guards… all of them fled. I am in charge there." He waited patiently for Josef to calm down before continuing with his story.

"My Maria sent to Dachau. I can't believe it," Josef repeated, then focused on his brother. "What? Then the castle is liberated, yes?"

"Not exactly. We are trapped there between an SS battalion and the Americans. We have older prisoners—French VIPs. Men, women, wives and husbands. Some are sick. It would be life-threatening to flee into the forest to hide."

Josef listened intently.

"We are twenty with few weapons," Kurt continued. "If we fled into the woods, many probably would not survive, so we decided to make a stand against the Panzers."

Josef stared at him. "The war could end any day, hour even."

"The Panzer unit seems determined to have a final battle and chose to defend the castle against the Americans." He looked around at Major Gangl's men. He saw no heavy weapons but did notice automatics and a machine gun. "It seems that they have nothing to lose."

"The SS will give their lives to save their honor," Josef replied. "But the prisoners… Why do they have to be with them? This I do not understand."

"The SS plans to kill all the prisoners—VIPs and servants… including me," he calmly told Josef. "They are ordered to fight to the end."

"Such insanity, with the war only days from ending," Josef said. "Yes, religious fanatics."

"What is your role in all this?"

"Maria and I have decided to defend them. Will you help us, brother?"

Josef looked hard into Kurt's eyes but made his decision quickly. "I, of course, will go with you, Kurt. My men… They want to go home to their families. I cannot commit them to more fighting. I must request volunteers."

"I did not know the Wehrmacht was so democratic." He smiled. "But yes, I understand."

Sergeant Krouse stepped forward to speak with his commander. "Major, I heard the captain and I'm with you. They are fools—renegades—who must be stopped… for our survival as well as the prisoners."

Josef looked at Krouse, smiled and nodded. He felt honored to have such a loyal soldier beside him. "Thank you, Sergeant. I would expect nothing less from a German soldier like you." He placed his hand on the sergeant's shoulder.

The older sergeant beamed with pride. "Ja, mein major," he said and then saluted.

"Please gather all the men behind this cottage so that I can speak with them."

"Ja, right away," Krouse said, saluted and moved forward to one of his men. He bent to whisper in the man's ear. The man nodded, and then got up to spread the word to the men.

The remaining soldiers of Major Josef Gangl's command gathered behind the small cottage. The major and Captain Schrader faced them together.

"Josef, you are a battalion commander. Where are the rest of your troops?" Kurt asked, not masking his surprise after seeing all Josef's men gathered together, and how few in number the soldiers were.

Josef looked proudly at him. "We are all that is left, Kurt. Three years of fighting. The rest? They are killed, wounded, captured, or simply ran away. They finally assigned us here because we are all Austrians."

Kurt understood. "Please explain to your men what I am asking," he said softly.

Josef looked at the group, at each man he had fought with for so long. Tears welled up. "Men, we have fought together, bled together, and for too many, died together." Choked up, he again paused. "Now, I ask that you go on one more mission with me. I know we decided that we would wait out the surrender here, but I am confronted with an extreme situation where the lives of unarmed civilians held as POWs are in immediate danger. They are French, Jew, and Austrian held by Hitler." He paused to judge reactions.

The soldiers said nothing. From their facial expression, Josef gathered that they did not understand how their situation involved them. "One of the prisoners is my wife, therefore, I must go. My brother, Captain Kurt Schrader has told me this."

His soldiers talked among themselves.

Kurt stepped forward to speak. He saw the looks on their faces. Who is this Hitler-loving bastard, they seemed to say. "I see you look at me, at an SS officer, and I know what you are thinking. But I have decided enough is enough. I have chosen to defend the castle and its prisoners against the Panzers. I believe that if we can hold them off for a day, the war will end." He stepped back to stand beside his brother and now, comrade in arms.

"I ask only for volunteers. Who will join me?" Josef asked, moving his gaze from man to man.

The men spoke among themselves. At first, no one stepped forward. Then, one by one, they did. Soon, all has volunteered. Josef and Kurt were relieved. The soldiers had mixed feelings about the new mission. Several were reluctant, but felt compelled, and others had nowhere to go. They knew if the SS captured them before the war's end, they could be shot as deserters. For all of them, it had been a very long war, and it showed on their faces, in their overwhelming fatigue.

"You are brave loyal soldiers. I thank you," Kurt said.

"Gather up all the weapons we have. We leave at once," Josef ordered, and everyone turned to leave.

Two hours later, a Kubelwagen, that when it ran, was Josef's staff car, pulled up in the courtyard of Schloss Itter. The vehicle, with barely enough fuel to reach the castle, was pockmarked with bullet holes. Its fenders hung on by a prayer. With Lieutenant Freerland behind the wheel, Major Gangl and Captain Schrader assisted a wounded man from the vehicle. Fifteen soldiers marched in formation behind the vehicle with Sergeant Krouse leading them.

The single injured soldier with them limped into the castle where he hoped to be cared for.

The two French generals and Reynaud stood in the courtyard and watched with a mix of surprise and worry. Josef excitedly followed the wounded man inside. He searched for his wife.

"Where's my wife?" he called. "Where is Maria Von Eickler?"

His question surprised the others inside. Finally, Bridget replied, "Here. She is over here."

"Maria!" Josef called, and then rushed to her.

Maria heard her name and looked up to see a German soldier running across the room. "Who? What is it?" she asked, not yet understanding.

"Maria, it is me, Josef."

Maria looked more carefully at the soldier and finally recognized him. At first, she could not believe it was him, her husband. She stood frozen to the stone floor. "Josef?" she said. "Is it really you?"

"Ja, my love," he replied. She moved toward him, first one step at a time, then faster. They embraced in the middle of the room.

"Oh, Josef, it is… It is you." They kissed.

The others looked on, most disbelieving something as beautiful as a reunion of husband and wife could happen at such a time. For several, watching instilled hope that soon something so joyous would happen to them.

"So long I've waited for this moment, my love. How I've thought of you and nothing else," Josef whispered.

"Ja, so long. You… I see how much you've changed. So thin. The war has done this to you," Maria said, breaking away from their embrace to look him over. "This war, Josef, what has it taken from us?" Overwhelmed with joy, she pulled him close to hold him tight. She never wanted to let go.

He, seeing her great loss of weight and her beautiful hair so short, frowned. He tenderly touched the scars on her arm. "Maria, who did this to you? The scars. Why are you in a SS prison? I don't understand. And Kurt?" He had so many questions for her.

She softly kissed him on the neck. "We have much to discuss, my love, but first… Has Kurt explained our dangerous predicament here?"

"He has and we have come to defend you. My men and I will do all that we can."

"Oh Josef, I'm so sorry you must risk your life yet again and to protect me." Maria rested her head on his chest. "I'm sorry," she repeated. "I cannot bear that you have suffered so."

"Things will work out. The war will end any day," he replied. "Maria, Kurt has told me that he rescued you from Dachau. How… ?" He stroked her face, and then touched her arm. "Who did that? Tell me. I must know."

She whispered, having to force the words from her mouth. "The Gestapo did it."

"They only know how to torture and kill. I saw this in France and even during the Rhine campaign—among the German people. They do this to their own people, too."

"I will tell you everything, but not now." Maria pulled away. "The war continues at Schloss Itter, my love."

Josef hesitated before allowing her to go. He looked at her, feeling angry and confused. Maria sensed his mood.

"Ja, later. Now we must prepare a defense and hope the Americans come before it is too late," he said, sounding committed. "Or the war quickly ends."

"We will stop them. I know it," she replied, clutching his hand tightly. Her words masked her lack of confidence in stopping the Panzers, but she had her husband beside her and that seemed for the moment to be enough.

CHAPTER 13

The handyman, Zvonimir Cuckovic, pedaled feverishly up the road toward Innsbruck. He did not know exactly where the Americans were, but he figured he had to run into them eventually. He had encountered refugees along the road but no soldiers of any army. Explosions seemed to surround him, and he saw an occasional airplane—American, he decided, but no fighting. He found that reassuring.

Cuckovic, a Czech Jew, was a carpenter and furniture maker by trade. The Germans at first found him useful building coffins for their many victims in and around Prague. Then in June 1942, following the assassination of the "Butcher of Prague", Reinhard Heydrich, the Nazis caught him in a major roundup of Jews and others destined for Auschwitz and surrounding camps. Only through the intercession of another notorious Nazi, Heinrich Himmler, who appreciated his craftsmanship, did he escape the death camps. He built several pieces of furniture for him. Himmler ordered that Cuckovic be sent to Schloss Itter. Ironically, Himmler had saved his life.

Rounding a sharp turn in the road, four soldiers jumped out of the woods and immediately surrounded him. All weapons pointed at Cuckovic's head.

Braking immediately and simultaneously raising his arms, he yelled, "No soldier, no soldier." He saw that the soldiers were American and was relieved.

"Yeah? Where do you think you're going?" the corporal in charge asked, still holding his M-1 in Cuckovic's face.

Cuckovic shook his head vigorously. "No English." He pointed back down the road excitedly. "SS, no good." He continued rapidly in his own language.

"What the hell is he trying to say?" a private asked. "It's not German, but something else."

"Just another refugee running from the Krauts," the corporal replied. He finally lowered his weapon, no longer concerned with the man.

Cuckovic rattled on, throwing in "SS" to hold their attention.

The private stood and listened to the man, who was growing more passionate as he spoke. "It's more than that, Corporal. He's not acting like the others we saw today. He's trying to tell us something important. I think we should get him back to the major, and find an interpreter, someone who speaks his lingo."

The corporal stood unmoved by the man or the private's argument. "Waste of time," he growled.

"The Krauts are ahead of us somewhere… near us. Maybe, he's warning us."

Hearing that, the corporal reluctantly gave in. "Yeah, why not. Better to be safe than sorry." He waved another private over. "Jennings, take this man back to the major."

"Yeah, no problem. Let's go," he said to Cuckovic. "I'm watching ya." He pointed his M-1 at him.

At the headquarters of the 23rd Tank Battalion of the 103rd Infantry, Major Kramer watched from the entrance to his tent as the young private walked up dragging an older civilian along, who in turn still pushed his bicycle.

"Sir," Private Jennings said when he stepped inside the tent with Cucovic minus the bike. "Corporal Billings thinks this man is telling us something. He keeps mumbling 'SS.'"

"Itter," the Czech said, excited.

Kramer stared at the two. "Lieutenant, figure out what language he's speaking.

It's not German."

The lieutenant walked over to the prisoner. "Speak," he said in German, the only other language he could speak, and not well.

Cuckovic looked at him and nodded. "Ja," he said, smiling. He proceeded to tell him he was Czech and had important information but needed to speak in his native language.

"Czech, eh? Send for Prusha," the lieutenant said to Private Jennings. "He speaks the language."

"Right away," Jennings replied and left the tent as quickly as he could. Within several minutes, Jennings returned with Sergeant Prusha in tow. "Sergeant, find out what this man is telling us."

"Right sir." Prusha spoke to the man in his language and Cuckovic seemed to understand.

Cuckovic spoke slowly, gesturing constantly.

When he had finished, Kramer, growing impatient, asked, "Well Sergeant, what the hell he say? Did you get it?"

"I did, Major."

"Well, goddamnit, tell me!"

"He says he is a camp inmate and serving important French prisoners at a castle just down the road. The SS guards have fled, but a Panzer Battalion is preparing to attack it and kill everyone. They want to fight in a final battle of the war. They need our help," Prusha said, translating. "He is begging us to help fight the SS."

Major Kramer nodded as Prusha translated and appeared to be considering the problem. He walked over to his map posted on his tent. "I see that the castle is outside our area of responsibility. I will need an order from Division to respond."

Prusha translated what Kramer had just said.

Cuckovic approached Kramer and with great passion exclaimed, "Please sir. Please help us now or surely, we will all die. I beg you." He grabbed Kamer's shoulders and looked directly into his blue eyes. It was not necessary that Prusha translate.

The Czech's plea for help moved Kramer. He understood that time was of the essence and immediately made a decision. "Lieutenant, get me Captain Lee. Hurry!"

"Yes, sir." He marched off to Lee's tank company.

Soon, six Sherman tanks, two jeeps, and a truck filled with soldiers departed from the battalion moving toward Schloss Itter. Many of Lee's men were African Americans led by Sergeant Glenn. Captain Lee was in the turret of the leading tank. The armor unit moved slowly down the road, not knowing who hid in the woods on both sides of the road.

Lee had sent out one of his jeeps earlier to reconnoiter the road between them and the castle. Cuckovic and Prusha rode with them.

About two miles out from the battalion command, a small band of partisans stepped out of the woods. The recon jeep halted and the men including Cuckovic bailed out. The leader of the partisan group waved at the Americans.

"America No. 1," their leader yelled and waved his rifle. Seeing the Americans watching him from the road, he continued to hold his weapon above his head and walk carefully, forward down the middle of the road. His comrades stayed behind, scattered along the road and in the woods. Reaching the American advance without incident, he began to speak.

"They're partisans, don't shoot them," Sergeant Glenn yelled from the ground. "Stop! SS on road chasing us. Over there," a partisan yelled in German, pointing down the road toward the castle.

Suddenly mortar rounds growled overhead. Everyone dove for cover in the woods. The jeep, emptied, took a direct hit, throwing steel in all directions.

"Holy shit," Sergeant Prusha mumbled under his breath. Cuckovic slowly crawled out from under a rotting log lying in the ditch when the barrage seemed to be over, Prusha beside him.

"SS," the partisan said. "We go." He had stepped out from behind a tree, where he had found cover. He ran back to his men.

"Johnson," Sergeant Glenn called. "Get over here."

From ten meters further down the road, a private looked up hearing his name called. "Ya, Sarge, I'm coming." He got up and ran to his team leader's position.

"Johnson, listen to me. Get back to the captain. Tell him we're under mortar attack and the Krauts are moving along the road. Go!"

Johnson, without saying a word, raced up the road, back to the company.

It didn't take long for Johnson to make contact with his company of tanks progressing more slowly up the road. He found the captain in the lead tank and quickly briefed him.

"We heard the explosions," Lee said. He considered whether to form the tanks into a defensive position or continue down the road. He stood on the tank and motioned to move out. He had made his decision. The Shermans revved up and lumbered down the road.

They soon passed the mangled jeep but not the recon patrol. Instead, they encountered the partisans, about six strong, entering the road from the safety of the forest.

They want to join us. They must be damn scared of the Krauts, Jack thought, watching them as they waved for rides atop the tanks. He saw they were well armed. The more the merrier, he decided.

"Hey Cap'n, where they coming from?" Lee's gunner asked, not having ever experienced civilians joining them so deep into Germany.

Lee looked down. "The Panzers are flushing them out of the woods. I think they want us to protect them." He pulled the cigar from his mouth and spit.

"Jeesus, the damn Tigers, I bet," Johnson said.

"Yup, get ready," Jack replied. "The bastards don't seem to understand the war is about over and they're whipped."

"Guess not. Hell with them. We'll kick their butts, too," his gunner replied from inside the tank. He did not sound overly confident.

"I like your attitude, Corporal." Lee gave him a thumbs-up. He saw a growing number of refugees passing them and wondered what it meant. Fleeing from something, he thought. "Halt," he ordered and raised his arm high. The formation quickly slowed to a halt. "Order the other jeep forward."

The jeep with its four riders pulled abreast of Lee, who was still standing on the tank.

"Whaddya need, Captain?" the senior enlisted man asked.

"I need you to find the boys. They're down the road somewhere. Find them and send them back."

"No problem."

"And get up ahead about two miles, scout around. The Krauts are up there somewhere. I want to know where."

"Gotcha sir."

"Hey, by the way, don't lose that damn jeep. It's the only one left."

"Don't worry none. I don't want to walk… to wherever hell we's going." He saluted.

The jeep moved off up the road, dodging refugees.

"Lieutenant," Jack called. "Get the men out of the truck and have them fan out on both sides of the road ahead of us. Take those partisans with you."

"Yes, sir."

Within seconds, soldiers were piling out of the truck. They divided into two squads and moved into the tree lines on both sides of the road. The black squad on one side and whites on the other side of the road, each squad following their leader. The tanks moved out slowly following their infantry.

Ahead of the column, the tanks heard gunfire, but they did not stop. Lee watched from the turret as the soldiers met up with the second recon team. The shooting stopped, and a team sergeant stepped out of the woods on the right side of the road and waved at Jack.

Jack halted the formation and waited for a report. "Yeah, what did you find?" he asked Sergeant Glenn.

"Some sniper fire but they shot and ran. I don't know where the main body is."

"Did you find the recon team?"

"Saw them. They're still moving forward—walking. I expect they'll get back soon. The little town can't be too far away."

He pulled out a worn, folded map and reviewed it. "According to my map, about a mile ahead, and the castle is just beyond it." He held it up for Glenn to see. He pointed at the castle, still chomping the cigar.

"Yup," Glenn agreed.

"But I need some intel on what we're walking into. Get those boys back here now. I need that report. And get those two Bohemians back here. I need them."

"Yessir."

The column continued plodding slowly down the road. Jack knew he was getting close to the town of Worgl, according to his map. The first recon patrol returned on foot, and Jack waited impatiently for a report.

"What's up ahead, Sarge?" he asked. Jack knew they were wasting valuable time.

"Flushed out a squad but they got away from us. I think the main force is moving toward that little town up ahead."

"Let me see," Jack looked again at his crumpled map. "The name is W-O-RG-L."

"Yes, sir, Worgl."

"That Czech we got with us is right. The Kraut battalion is moving for the castle," Jack said. "I need you and your men to snoop around the town. Find out who the hell is there. Be careful, damn careful you don't run into the whole battalion. Ya got that?"

"Got it."

"Go."

The sergeant hurried off down the road to find his team just as Cuckovic and Prusha walked toward Besotten Jenny. Everyone watched them approach.

"The cap'n looking for ya, Prusha," an infantryman told him and pointed to Lee.

They got to the tank as Jack gave orders to Pride and the other commanders.

Everyone held up along the road awaiting orders.

"Hey Prusha, ask him how large this Worgl is," Jack said when the two reached his tank. "And does he know if there are German troops garrisoned there." Impatience shaded each word.

Prusha did as requested, and turned to the Czech. There was a brief exchange and he turned back to Lee. "Captain, he says the town is small. He's never been there but heard talk from the guards who got some supplies from there. Could be German soldiers there but he doesn't know."

Jack looked hard at the Czech, thinking. "Yeah, okay. Get back to your squad and take him with you," Jack said. "He looks like he's hungry. Give him a couple cartons of C's. We got plenty."

Cuckovic, who could not even remember when he'd had a decent meal, beamed with joy.

"Right." Prusha grabbed Cuckovic's arm, and they left.

Captain Lee and his tank company departed with greater speed, arrived at the outskirts of Worgl within minutes. He sent out an advance to recon the village.

The recon team quickly returned and reported what they observed to Jack. They had spotted the SS moving around in the village. They counted about a dozen, but they knew there could easily be more. They saw that the SS were taking fire from inside houses. Sporadic gunfire came from the far side but near the village circle. Most importantly, they saw no Panzer armor deployed in or around Worgl. Jack immediately took action. He gave a hand signal to four tank crews, and they labored slowly forward. He pointed to how he wanted each Sherman deployed.

The infantry followed close behind each tank. The remainder of the company—two tanks—stayed on the outskirts of the village to act as a blocking force.

Deployed, the tanks remained silent, but the supporting infantry spread out, with occasional shooting but the targets were few. Soon, all gunfire ceased. Jack saw civilians he assumed were partisans walking down the street. SS soldiers were not seen anywhere.

He called Lieutenant Bar up with a wave of his hand. Bar jumped from his tank and ran over to Besotten Jenny.

"Yes, sir."

"I got to move to the castle, Bar. I think that's where the Krauts plan to strike and soon."

Bar listened while watching the half dozen armed civilians approached them. "Who the hell you think they are?"

"More from the same partisan group we have riding with us," Jack replied. "Use them with the infantry. They appear to be well armed and motivated."

"Sir?"

"I'm leaving four tanks here to defend the village with most of our infantry. Deploy them to hold off an attack probably from that direction." He pointed up the road. "Don't know how many yet."

Bar looked around and nodded. "Lots of heavy stone here. Should be easy to hold them off, depending on how many Tigers and how long." He spat on the cobblestone and adjusted his cartridge belt.

"Don't be a hero. This war is too close to being over," Jack said. "If you have to, if there's too many, pull back into those woods." He paused. "Hey, don't destroy the damn town. Defend it. It's not Berlin."

Bar looked at the woods surrounding town. "I'm moving up to the castle. Good luck." "Thanks, Jack." He returned to his tank.

Jack waved to another Sherman. "Move out," he called and the two tanks with infantry riding on top turned and rumbled up the road to Castle Itter, leaving the truck hidden in the village. Five hundred yards before the castle, they spotted a roadblock in the distance on the intersection of two roads. They halted. Jack sent out two men to assess. A few minutes later, they returned.

"Cap'n, looks like four men are holding the intersection, mostly traffic control, I'd say."

"Hmmm, what say we drop a round on them? Give 'em a scare." He looked down at his gunner. "Whenever you're ready, Sammy, fire for effect."

Within seconds, the main gun fired. The tank jerked from the recoil. The high explosive round landed only yards from the intersection but off in the trees. Two of his infantrymen fired their M-1s. They laughed as the defenders ran off into the woods without firing a shot.

"Good show, Sammy. It did the trick." He waved at the second tank commander. He jumped off his Sherman and walked over to Jack.

"Now what, Cap'n?"

"I'm leaving you here to cover the intersection with the Negro squad from First Platoon. They hit you with force don't dawdle. Give them all you got; make a lot of noise, then get the hell back to the village. That understood?"

"Yessir."

"Good luck… and stay alert. They could hit you from anywhere." Jack tapped the steel with his hand and Besotten Jenny growled forward.

Captain Lee in the one tank with his remaining soldiers, including Cuckovic, moved up the road the short distance to the castle. His infantry now walked behind the tank flanking it on both sides of the road to move through the woods hoping to flush out any enemy soldiers. A hundred yards before reaching the clearing in front of the castle, Lee stopped the tank and several of his men jumped on. Everyone looked up to admire the old castle, seeing its high walls tower over the clearing. Behind it the mountains rose.

"Castle Itter," Jack announced, still idling in the meadow. "Damn! Those walls are high," he muttered, impressed. Looking through binoculars, he panned the great stone fort, considering how to defend it against an armor attack. He saw only the road they rode up on, and one entrance—through that arched passage. *If their numbers are few, we have a chance, if not, maybe an hour tops, and they're inside,* he thought, still observing the layout.

Besotten Jenny continued to idle in the meadow in front of Itter. *A major frontal assault supported by Tigers and .88s, and we're dead.*

"Stop on the bridge," he ordered the driver.

CHAPTER 14

At the ancient stone bridge immediately in front of the castle, the tank stopped, and Jack jumped onto the stone. He walked over and looked down at the narrow, deep ravine. He smiled at seeing the depth of it. It'll take a while to get across it from this single point of entry, he thought, and they got to take the bridge. It's the only way into the castle. That was a good thing. He tried to smile.

"Hey Sarge," he called up to the TC in the turret.

His tank commander popped up from the turret and looked down at him. "Yeah?" he asked.

"Get everybody off then turn around and back onto the bridge. Stop right smack in the middle."

"Right, Jack," Sergeant Miller replied. "Everyone out but Jake."

The crew spilled out of Besotten Jenny. The half-dozen infantrymen riding on top—mostly his NCOs—jumped off, followed by the tankers. The Sherman backed off the bridge, spun around, then slowly backed back on.

"Aim it out that way," Jack yelled, then pointed at the narrow road coming out of the forest. "They'll come from that direction. They have to with those heavy tanks."

When the work was completed, Miller and the gunner hopped off and joined Jack and the others. Jack figured he had about nineteen men, including eight coming up the road behind him. Cuckovic and a couple of partisans stood to watch the tank perform.

Jack looked up to marvel at the great stone fortification. He saw walls of solid granite at least two feet thick. Impressed, he shook his head and smiled. He knew from reports it had been constructed six hundred years earlier. Must be ten stories from bottom to top, he reckoned, and I think this ravine was actually a moat. Fascinated, he lit a fresh cigar, and took a second to admire the fine and intricate masonry work. Better job than they're doing with those skyscrapers, he thought.

Back to the present. "Okay, spread out and move through the wide stone gate," he said to his men. He had to be cautious despite the Czech's assurances.

Everyone did as ordered. Weapons at the ready, they moved slowly forward through the gate. Jack led the way.

Reynaud, Schrader, and Gangl left the main hall and excitedly walked across the courtyard to greet the approaching Americans.

Jack watched the three men walk across the courtyard. "Now that's a scary group, ain't it?" he whispered to Sergeant Miller. They saw a Wehrmacht soldier, an SS soldier, and a much older man in civilian clothes walk toward them. When they were face to face, he decided the two Germans were no less apprehensive of him. After all, they had been adversaries a few days earlier.

They greeted each other with handshakes and forced smiles. Lee's men gathered around the four men, not really knowing what to do. They had lowered their weapons but had not slung their rifles... just in case.

The Czech was overjoyed, nodding and smiling. He had succeeded in his mission.

Reynaud carefully examined the group of soldiers and partisans with a look of growing concern.

"Where are the rest of your forces, Captain?" he asked.

Jack looked at him, pulled the cigar from his mouth, spit, then smiled broadly and confidently.

"This is it, Frenchy. The rest are on the road around Worgl," he replied. "Anyway, we're the American Army. My boys'll take care of your troubles." He smiled. "Now, who the hell are ya and how many we got here? And weapons, that sort of thing. You understand what I'm saying?"

"Perfectly," Reynaud replied. "And the name is Reynaud, Paul Reynaud. I am the former Premier of the French Republic. Before the Nazi invasion."

Jack spit again and re-lit his cigar. "Gotcha," he replied. "French."

Reynaud watched with disgust but said nothing. He refused to allow the slight to hinder their efforts.

"Who the hell is in charge here? You, Mr. Rey-Naud?" He looked at the Frenchman then slowly to Schrader and Gangl. At first, the situation was awkward and intense. *Fraternizing with two men I should probably arrest as POWs or worse*, Jack thought, amused.

Josef stepped forward. "I am, and I speak English very well."

"Goddamn, a German infantry officer." He looked at the rank. "A major, eh?"

Where are the rest of your men? I don't see very many here?"

"We are few and all that remain, but we are committed to defending this place and the prisoners."

Jack puffed on his cigar, sizing up the Wehrmacht major. "Gangl... you said your name was Gangl."

"Yes, Josef Gangl."

Lee's men listened quietly to the conversation, their weapons relaxed. They were curious and taken aback by everything, much like their commander.

Maria with the others—prisoners and inmates—watched the scene unfold through the large windows. For some reason, she felt good about her husband speaking to the American on equal terms, not as captor to prisoner. *As it should be*, she decided.

"How many of you are there? Soldiers and civilians?" Jack asked.

Josef thought a moment. "About twenty, I think, and twenty civilians. My men are all combat tested. The civilians are prisoners held by the SS... until just yesterday. They are mostly old, some in poor health, but all can hold a weapon if needed."

"Weapons?"

"I've been here only a couple of hours before you arrived, but I've surveyed them. One MP-40, half my men have automatic weapons, a couple of rockets. The civilians have pistols and rifles with some ammunition, nothing heavier. We're still searching for more ammo."

"How long you think we can hold out?"

Josef smiled and shook his head. "Not long," he replied. "When will more of you Americans arrive?"

Jack shrugged. "Good question. I hope that they are only hours behind us, but resistance, breakdowns… Who knows? A day, maybe less." He looked around slowly. "By the way, what happened to the guards here?"

"Ha! It seems they woke to find all the guards gone, gone except for Captain Schrader, who is only temporarily assigned here. He was wounded fighting the Russians and is convalescing here. We are very fortunate to have him on our side."

Jack looked to Schrader. "I see. Fighting on the front lines or doing something else?" He found it almost unbelievable he had an SS captain joining him to fight other SS. He decided to accept it for now, but he knew he would have to keep an eye on him.

"He was a company commander," Josef replied.

"Okay, let's leave it at that," Jack replied. He needed every man to fight. "Major, shall we take a look at our defenses?" Jack turned to walk through the castle. "Will you show me?"

"Of course." He and Reynaud led the way.

Josef saw that the American was not convinced of their determination to hold the castle. "Captain, I want you to understand Captain Schrader, my men, and I are committed to defending this castle… even against Germans."

Jack did not reply.

"I have a very important reason." "What is that, Major?"

"My wife was captured by the Gestapo. She is here, and I will willingly give my life to protect her even against my comrades, ah former comrades, as will Captain Schrader. As it happens, we are all childhood friends."

That surprised Jack. "I greatly appreciate hearing that. Those are important reasons to risk your lives."

"And I might add, Captain, that as a German officer, I have always operated strictly by the rules of the Geneva Convention. I served in France when you invaded, and have fought Americans and British since, as have my men. That is, what's left of them."

"This will be highly irregular, but we will do it."

Josef appreciated this American's spirit. He's a fighting man like me, he thought.

Or as I was.

The three men walked through the main hall where Jack was able to see all who would fight beside him. He removed the cigar from his mouth and spit, missing Reynaud's shoe by inches. Looking around, he saw soldiers and armed civilians engaged in preparations for the coming battle. He saw that even the few women he saw were armed, except for the much older one, who acted like she was in charge. She acts too haughty for a prisoner, he thought. I wonder what her story is.

Everyone shook the Americans' hands and welcomed them, but foremost on their minds was the upcoming battle. They were excited at being liberated, but fear was written on each face. Seeing focus and determination from them impressed Jack. He liked that. It'll be a short but tough fight. Their survival is at stake, and they know it. That's good, he thought, hoping it would give them an edge.

Two women, the older one, and a much younger and very attractive one, approached him. He was struck by her beauty, even in the faded brown shift the young woman wore.

"You saved us, Captain," the older woman said, shaking his hand again. "My name is Marie Cailliau. I am the sister of General Charles De Gaulle, commanding Free French forces, a name I'm sure you recognize."

"Heard the name," Jack replied, not impressed.

"I can speak for everyone when I say we are greatly appreciative. If we survive this ordeal, I am certain my brother will reward you."

"No reward necessary ma'am," Jack replied. "Just doing my job." He turned to the younger woman. He saw immediately that she had a Luger tucked into an ammunition belt around her shift, with a bandolier of ammo strung across her chest. "And you are?" Jack asked, impressed. He extended his hand.

Maria smiled and took his hand. "My name is Maria Von Eickler. I am one of the camp inmates brought here to serve the prisoners. I hate the SS bastards, and now, I am prepared to give my life fighting them," she said with great emotion.

Jack was taken aback by her zeal, finding it a little difficult to understand. "You were brought from Dachau?" He saw that she wore clothing much as he saw days earlier at the main camps.

"Yes, I was to be shot there, but an old friend, Captain Schrader, rescued me." "What could someone so beautiful be accused of doing?" he asked with too much interest.

"I was accused of treason," Maria replied directly. She saw she had his full attention. "The Gestapo caught me rescuing Russian and American flyers. Earlier in the war, they would have summarily executed me, but mostly because of family connections, they decided to get rid of me by sending me to Dachau to die. That is, following days where they tortured me."

"Thank you for telling me your story," he replied, mesmerized by her actions in addition to her beauty. "I think you are a hero." Her passion for fighting the German SS became more understandable to him.

"To some, perhaps," Maria said, looking around the room. It confused her to see so many men wearing different uniforms. "I must find my husband." She turned abruptly and walked away, leaving Jack standing there.

Marie Cailliau, standing near, overheard the conversation but said nothing. She and Jack watched as she grabbed Major Gangl's hand. Jack turned and left the older woman standing alone. He was indifferent to who her brother was.

"I see that you two know each other. What luck to find each other in such circumstances," Jack said, having followed Maria. He felt moved by their show of affection.

"The major is my husband whom I have not seen in more than two years," Maria replied. "But to be brought together in such a place… " She rested her head on Josef's shoulder.

"Life plays terrible tricks, so I think you are very fortunate. War, it seems to me, leaves little room for love."

Maria looked at Jack. "Captain, we are Austrians, but I am fully prepared to fight to the death beside my husband against Hitler's horde. Please do not mock us."

"I would never mock someone of your moral strength and determination, Madame Von Eikler."

Bridget and Cuckovic brought out bottles of wine—all that remained in their stores.

"A toast," General Gamelin announced. "To our liberation."

"Wine we have, Captain, but, I'm afraid our pantry is empty," Gamelin informed Lee.

Jack nodded. "We can easily remedy that." With a smile, he took one of the glasses offered by Bridget.

"I propose a toast to the United States of America and President Roosevelt for our rescue. To our liberation," Gamelin said loudly so all could hear.

"And to the U.S. Army," Jack said. "But I must tell you. President Roosevelt died about a month ago. Harry Truman is now our president."

"Then we salute him." Everyone present, including six of Lee's men, held their glasses high in toast.

"Here! Here! To our American liberators," the prisoners and inmates chanted.

The German soldiers present were understandably quiet, but polite.

"To General De Gaulle and the Free French," Paul Reynaud toasted.

Marie Cailliau beamed. "Yes, yes to my brother and his soldiers," she toasted. Everyone but the Fascists present raised their glasses. Jack noticed the two men with their heads bowed.

Cuckovic passed bottles of wine around to all. Americans, French, Germans, and Austrians. All engaged in limited conversations—mostly forced—as distrust ran high, especially among the Americans and Wehrmacht soldiers.

After only one drink, Jack set his glass down. "Major, shall we examine our defenses?" he asked Gangl.

"Ja, of course, Captain," Josef replied. "And I want Captain Schrader to accompany us. He knows much more about this place and also has combat experience."

Jack nodded, but by his facial expression, was not too pleased with the SS officer joining them.

Kurt, seeing the reaction said, "I understand Captain that you do not trust me, but I do have great knowledge of this place, having been here since February and charged with security."

"Lead the way, Captain," Jack said.

Kurt gave the other two a complete but quick tour of Castle Itter. When they reached the high outer walls, Josef pointed across the moat below to the tree line. "Great fields of fire from this point, wouldn't you say, Captain?"

Kurt smiled. "If you have good marksmen."

"We'll place our best sharpshooters here and over there," Jack continued, trying to overlook the SS officer's comment.

"I agree," Josef said.

Having reviewed the upper walls, they returned to the main hall. "Now to the gate," Kurt said and led the way through the courtyard.

"The gate, I'm certain, will be the main focus of their attack. Here and up there we must place most of our men," Josef said.

Jack quietly agreed. He was little experienced in defensive positions. He and his men had been on the offensive since landing in France.

"Our tank, Captain? Where should it be placed?" Josef asked.

Jack jerked his head. He was not accustomed to having a German soldier discuss placement of his tanks.

"Where will I place the tank? It will stay there on the bridge facing down the road. Tactically and practically, I see no better position. Besotten Jenny can hold her own," he said proudly.

"Sorry if I offended you, Captain," Josef replied quickly. "Will that halt any armor advance?"

"Remember, the Panzers are tough. I served with them for three years in Russia," Kurt added. "They have the best—Tigers."

Jack bristled. "Do you think they're so tough they can push the tank off the bridge while under heavy fire?"

"I see your point," Kurt added. "Ja, good," Josef replied quickly.

"Captain, you said you have other tanks. Where are they?" Kurt asked with concern.

"I have my other tanks deployed on the road and around the village where they have more room to maneuver against the bigger Tigers," he replied testily.

"Why? Here will be the center of battle," Kurt said.

"The Panzers must also take and hold the village to protect their flank." "I see," Josef said. "Can your men hold them off there?"

Jack again bristled. "My boys will hold the village. They have proven to be excellent fighters against your boys. They have encountered similar tactical situations, Major. You may be familiar with them—the Vosges Mountains and Neustat."

The two Austrians wisely did not respond. The three men stood in front of the Sherman staring into the forest. Maria stood under the arched gate watching and listening. Paul Reynaud was beside her. He, too, listened, hoping the American knew what he was doing.

"Their plan is our only hope, Maria," he said, speaking softly. "It must work." "I understand," she replied.

"Your buddies are already in those trees watching us," Jack said. "You know that, don't you Captain Schrader." Jack could sense the enemy presence. Tomorrow, early, he decided, but said nothing. First, we complete our preparations.

"I know that, Captain," Kurt replied. "And we will be ready for them."

"We have to be," Jack said. The three men returned to the main hall. Josef looked for Maria while Kurt took the steps to a floor above. Jack stood in the doorway gazing out through the arched gate. He considered his opponent. What do you want here? The war is over for you, he thought.

He had earlier heard the latest war news. According to all reports, the Allies were advancing on all fronts. The Americans, British and French in the west and the Russians in the east. Hitler was dead by suicide in his bunker in Berlin. What the hell is the point of a German attack, and in this remote place? Those thoughts rolled over repeatedly in his head.

CHAPTER 15

Two hundred yards away, on a heavily forested mountain near the road overlooking the castle, Major Speers watched. Looking through binoculars, he saw the three soldiers in front of the American tank. He was mostly interested in seeing an American—the enemy—standing among his former comrades—traitors. What does that mean? he wondered. His men had scattered the refugees clogging the road, giving his tanks free movement toward Itter, and they were back on schedule.

He had hoped Captain Wimmer and his men would open the gate for them so they could simply march in and take up defensive positions, but that was not going to happen. He tried to mask his anger and frustration. Good German soldiers will now die because of their cowardice, he thought, wondering why the American advance did not kill Captain Wimmer. He's a coward, Speers concluded, scoffing. He probably ran before they even reached the castle.

Regardless, Speers knew the castle defender's numbers were few. Maybe fifty, he thought. Reports from his recon indicated that the primary American armored force was deployed around the village, and it consisted of only a few Shermans, a tank he held in contempt.

He saw only the one American tank at the castle. We'll easily dispose of it when it approaches the trees. He liked that. Then we will march into the castle. "Lieutenant, come here," he ordered.

"Ja, Herr Major," the younger man replied, moving to stand beside Speers. "Are the tanks ready?"

"Ja, they are prepared to go." "My infantry?"

"Ja, they are in the trees within meters of the castle."

"Good, good. Tell everyone to stay the night in place. No fires, cold rations.

We will attack early. Send me my commanders."

"Ja," he saluted and prepared to leave, but suddenly remembered. "Sir, the three deserters we caught this afternoon among the refugees? What are your orders?"

Speers turned, pausing to consider. "Bring Captain Wimmer to me. Shoot the others for desertion. We will make an example of them in front of the men."

We are soldiers of the Third Reich, he thought. We are well-trained and experienced professionals. This is what we do. We fight. Speers had told his men that repeatedly during the past three years. He was not going to allow this drunken deserter to get away with his bad behavior, which was contrary to everything he believed. To him, it did not matter that the war was almost over. A good German soldier must hold his post until relieved… or killed.

The lieutenant nodded and left. "One more thing."

"Ja?"

"I want the officer who recognized Wimmer here, too." The lieutenant turned to disappear into the trees.

Soon, he returned with both Wimmer and the recon lieutenant. Wimmer was marched at gunpoint with his wrists tightly bound. The prisoner walked off balance but otherwise was not impaired.

"Captain Wimmer, the officer in charge at Schloss Itter. The man who held high-ranking French prisoners for Himmler. Are you not he who was to allow us entrance to fight the Americans?"

Captain Wimmer nodded, his head bowed.

"Speak!" Speers ordered, standing directly in front of him. Speers' commanders stood in a half circle around them. They said nothing.

"Ja," Wimmer uttered quietly.

"Do you know that the American Army now holds the castle? Do you understand that to take it, I will lose many brave, honorable soldiers? All because you abandoned your post and deserted." He struck him across the head with his baton.

Wimmer grimaced but said nothing.

"Speak," he ordered again. "What do you say for yourself, Captain Wimmer?

It may be your last chance to speak."

Upon hearing that, Wimmer looked up. "Have mercy, comrade. The war is almost over. This is unnecessary. We were only going home… to our wives and families."

"All of us want to go home to our families, but honor… the honor of being Schutzstaffel, the best and the bravest. We cannot go home until the war is over. Our honor demands that. You, Captain, are a coward and a deserter."

Wimmer said nothing.

"Lieutenant, what should we do with this deserter? I will allow you to determine this man's fate."

The lieutenant stared at their prisoner, but he wasted no time in making a decision. "Give him what he deserves, just like the others. Shoot him."

"You've heard your sentence, Captain Wimmer. What do you have to say?" "I will fight with you if you let me live. I will be in the front line."

"Ha! I will never allow a person like you to fight beside brave and honorable soldiers of the Third Reich. You will not die an honorable death," Major Speers replied. "Take him."

"Ja, Herr Major." The lieutenant grabbed Wimmer and pushed him along.

Speers looked to his commanders still standing there.

"We will speak no more about this," he said. "Gentlemen, are your men prepared? We will assault the castle at daybreak. Is everything ready?"

Each nodded in the affirmative.

"Excellent. Then by midday, we will be lunching in Schloss Itter waiting for the rest of the Americans. Heil Hitler!" He raised his arm.

"Heil Hitler!" Each man said loudly and gave the stiff-arm salute. "Remember, we fight for our honor."

"Sir, our supply of ammo is low. Where is our supply train?"

Speers looked at him, thinking, Such a stupid question. "Find good targets, Captain. You have all that you will get," he replied. There was no supply train.

"Lieutenant, come here," he motioned for his aide.

"Ja, Herr Major," the young man replied, hurrying to him. "Alert all units. No fires."

"Ja." He paused before leaving. "Ja, a question?"

"Herr Major, how do we handle captives?"

"The traitors who fight against us will be shot along with the French captives." "The American prisoners?"

"They will be treated as prisoners of war," Speers replied. "We will negotiate with the larger American force when it arrives. Their lives for ours."

"Sir, I thought this was a fight to the end to uphold our honor. Have things changed?"

"We will show the Americans how real German soldiers fight," he replied. "But Captain, it is always good to have a bargaining chip. Any more questions?" There were none. "Good, then by midday we will be lunching on American rations in Schloss Itter." He hoped saying that would motivate his men. They nodded, smiled politely and began to file out toward their tanks.

"Dismissed… and gentlemen, good luck." He wanted no more discussion.

Major Speers watched his commanders return to their units. His aide remained.

"Lieutenant, one more thing. Tonight, when the men and tanks are in position, begin the mortar barrage and increase it early in the morning. Focus on the courtyard. Harassment should keep them off balance."

"Ja, Herr Major." He saluted and left.

Suddenly, they heard the crack, crack of several rifles. Both men turned to look in the direction of the road. Joaquin Speers shrugged and left to inspect positions. "There is no room for cowards and traitors in the German Army," he whispered, mostly to himself.

CHAPTER 16

Darkness came quickly to the woods and mountains of Austria. Maria and Josef were in a room on the upper floor of the castle she had prepared earlier. This night was for them as husband and wife. Josef ordered all lights in the castle turned off. The small room was bathed in shadows.

The couple stood awkwardly looking at each other. Maria had removed her cartridge belt and bandolier of ammo. They lay on the floor. Josef noticed immediately, not accustomed to seeing his wife armed.

"Oh Josef, my love, you've changed so much. The war… " She touched him softly on the cheek.

"And you? A pistol?" he said, looking at the weapon on the floor. A forced smile masked his concern.

Explosions from mortar rounds pounded the courtyard but some found their way to the roof and against the walls. They made little impact on the castle's heavy stone construction, but the noise was nerve-wracking and disturbing.

"Maria, I've thought of you every day," he said softly, pulling her close. He kissed her lightly at first, then much more passionately. She fell into his arms. "It has been so long, my darling." They fell back on the small bed. Its mattress was stuffed with straw from the fields, and they both giggled like children. "Is this really you? I thought I'd never see you again."

The explosions continued, but for the moment, neither noticed.

She began to unbutton his uniform. "I've thought so long about this moment.

What I would do. How I would touch you." She helped him with his tunic.

Josef looked at the woman beside him, at the ragged brown shift. "Maria, why?

I don't understand."

She pulled off her shift to reveal her nudity… and her scars. "Please, my love, don't talk, not now. Touch me, touch me everywhere. Tonight is for us."

Josef touched a mostly healed scar, then bent to kiss her small but firm breast. Maria leaned her head back and smiled. She pushed his head lower.

"I must know what happened."

"Later, much later," she whispered with growing passion. She opened her legs to him. "Yes, yes, that's it," she moaned softly. "More, please more."

Slowly, he moved his head up to her breasts, smothering her with kisses.

"Let me please you. Oh, so long," she whispered raising her naked body. She reached down, touched him, and felt him harden. She unbuttoned his trousers, pulled them open and reached for him. Holding him in her hands, she bent to kiss him.

Josef's breathing increased. He stood to throw off his trousers. For a brief second he looked at her, his beautiful wife, and smiled. "I missed you so much," he said then covered her with his body.

Later, they lay naked in the darkness, holding each other. The explosions continued outside. They stared into the darkness above them. They knew their future was unknown and perilous. But tonight they had each other even if for short hours.

"My darling, tell me your story. How could they take you to Dachau?" He had to know more.

Maria closed her eyes to bring back the memories she'd fought so hard to suppress. "I helped an American pilot. An airplane was shot down near our estate. They had parachuted and landed in our meadow. One man—the pilot—was alive. I could not allow him to die. Oh, Josef, he even had a German name—Schwartz."

Josef smiled. He knew how sensitive the woman he married was and he also knew she could neither allow the man to die or turn him in.

"Last fall, the war had dragged on for too long. So much suffering. The boys returning with horrible wounds, the funerals. I had to do something, anything to end it so I joined the resistance. Do you hate me?"

"Oh Maria, you took a dangerous risk. The Gestapo… they're merciless. But I'm not angry. I, and my men, too, have had enough of this war. We came to Worgl to surrender to the Americans." They hugged, tears flowing. "How did they catch you?" he asked.

"The Home Guard, someone, a servant I think, told them, and they came to the estate. They barged into the house while the American was still there. They took him and arrested me. Rolf protested but he could not free me. 'Treason,' they said."

"Old men and boys controlled by the Gestapo. They do whatever they're told to do." He shook his head.

"The Gestapo took me. They beat me, cut me, shaved my head and said I was a spy for the Americans." She paused, fighting to hold back her anger and her tears. "Oh, Josef, one of them—their commander—raped me." Her rage engulfed him.

Josef embraced her tightly, fighting to hold back his emotions. "Maria, I'm so sorry." He knew saying that was not enough but could find no other words to console her.

"See my scars." She showed him the healed wounds on her arms, back, and buttocks. "The bastards did that."

"The Gestapo, murderers, thugs. If I had been there, I would have stopped them or died trying," he said, finding words.

"Then they decided to send me to Dachau. The Russians were getting close, and they knew the villagers would not accept an execution there in the public square. Rolf would never allow it and they fear him. So they sent me to Dachau to be shot."

"Where Kurt found you and brought you here?"

"Ja, he saw me after I got off the train." Maria looked at him, tears still streaking down her cheeks. "Now, Josef, my love, what do we do?"

"Tomorrow, we fight them, and if we live, the Americans will come, but I fear we are not in control of the situation. I think the war has discovered the old castle."

"My love, we must believe in the future," she said. "And I feel more in control than before with you beside me. Soon the war will end, and we can resume our lives. We must believe that."

"I love your strength." He smiled.

She curled up closer to him. "Remember that summer just after Hitler's soldiers marched into Austria? We were so happy—with Kurt. We spent the summer at Rolf's summerhouse high in the mountains. Everything seemed so far away. Oh Josef, we were so much in love."

"A hundred years ago, or so it seems," he said, the memories springing to life once again. He had cherished them all during the fighting but had to bury them deep if for no other reason than his own sanity.

August 1, 1939

A younger Josef and Maria playfully frolicked in the cold blue lake in the mountains while Kurt sat under a tree reading and watching them. They were naked. Their clothes were stacked in three separate piles under a large Oak.

Maria challenged Josef. "Catch me and I'll give you a reward," she called to him.

She dove, swimming toward the far shore.

Kurt set aside his book and stood to watch.

Josef dove deep, surfaced only feet away and then swam hard to catch her.

Maria laughed as she backstroked, her naked body brown from a summer in the sun. Josef gained on her, and then caught her. He reached out to pull her under. Kurt laughed at their antics.

Josef wrapped his arms around her legs, swimming closer to press his body against hers. Maria did not struggle but relaxed in his arms. They surfaced bound in one another's arms.

Kurt, still standing, clapped. "Marvelous," he yelled, obviously entertained. "I love you," Josef whispered in her ear. His body still pressed against hers.

Maria felt him hard against her stomach. She did not know what to do, but she did not force him away. "Oh Josef," she whispered back.

"I want you now. Over there," he said, pressing his lips against her breast.

"But Kurt," she replied. "He will ignore us."

"No, I cannot, not here, now," Maria said, still in his embrace. "I want to feel you inside me, but… " Suddenly, she pushed off with her knees, and swam as fast as she could toward the bank. Reaching shore, she lifted herself out of the water, turned, and yelled. "Marry me first."

Josef laughed, racing after her. He reached shore only seconds behind Maria. Wanting to join in on the fun, Kurt dove into the lake and swam toward them.

They watched as he came closer.

He pulled himself from the water and walked over to sit beside the two lovers. "Maria, you're such a trollop," he said, laughing. "You're driving poor Josef mad with your behavior."

"The three of us… We will run away to Vienna or even Paris," she announced. "We will be Bohemians. I will write poetry with Josef. Kurt will read his Nazi propaganda, and the three of us will sit in the outdoor cafes."

"Yes," Kurt replied. "We will talk philosophy with whomever. I like that."

"But never politics with you," Josef said. 'Then we would only argue or fight. This Hitler of yours is not good, and he will plunge the world into war if he continues his demands."

"He wants to make Germany great again, and we are Germans, too," Kurt replied. "You listen to too much BBC."

"Boys," Maria said and kissed both on the cheeks. "Then it's Paris, the city of peace and love."

"To Paris," Kurt replied. He jumped up and ran toward the water.

Josef quietly watched him dive into the water. Wondering about Kurt, he knew trouble was on the horizon even then, and he wondered what his stepbrother would do. Those concerns deeply troubled him.

Josef's mother had married Kurt's father following his father's early death. Rolf brought Maria into their household when she was only an infant. Her parents both died when the flu epidemic struck eastern Austria following the Great War when thousands perished. Rolf raised her as a sister to the two boys, and as they were part of the Austrian landed gentry, they were mostly isolated from the struggles of the ordinary people. Rolf expected the two boys to rule Austria one day.

"Come, my love," Maria said, pulling Josef to his feet. "I will race you across."

He beat her, but only by inches, and stood on the edge of the water to offer his hand. She enjoyed the sight of his naked body. He tried to hide his nakedness. Kurt watched them with envy from the water. He also had feelings for Maria and she knew.

Maria smiled at the wonderful memories. Both agreed that was another, more innocent time.

Neither could sleep as the bombardment pounded at the courtyard and rattled the old windowpanes.

"Josef, that summer was so wonderful, then both of you went off to university. I waited each day for a letter. The war, the horrible war, changed everything for us."

"My stepfather? What did he do when you were arrested?"

"Oh Josef, it was horrible. He tried to fight them, but he was easily overpowered. You know how frail he was?"

"Was?"

"He's dead," Maria whispered, holding his hand tightly. "I'm so sorry."
"How?"

"It's all my fault, I'm so sorry." She wept softly, her head on his shoulder. "I heard later. His heart... after. He didn't make it. Oh Josef, it's all my fault," she repeated.

"The Nazis, they killed him, not you," Josef said, feeling the great loss of his stepfather. A good and fair man who will be missed, he thought sadly.

"I should have been more discreet. They have spies everywhere and we were betrayed. But Rolf was innocent of my doings. An old man who hurt no one."

"Did you tell Kurt about his dad?"

"I told him only that he died of a heart attack. We knew that with a weak heart and many problems, his time was limited."

"Does Kurt know about the American pilot and the trouble it caused Rolf?" "No," she said. "Please don't hate me, but I don't know how to tell him when he has saved my life."

"I could never hate you, my love. Even when we were children, I loved you.

Nothing you say would make me love you less."

"I learned that the Gestapo had been watching me for several weeks. Someone must have told them of my activities. Even before the wounded pilot. I think neighbors couldn't accept that I despised Hitler and his war."

"Everything became worse as the war turned against us."

"The repression, food and fuel rationing became unbearable. The police, then the Home Guard and the Gestapo... They watched us. The mass arrests of Jews and people like me began in '43, I think. Everything was so bad." Maria rambled on. "Rolf protected me. He used his money and influence to help people, pay off the Home Guard, but then the Gestapo took control."

"Rolf, the rich aristocrat."

"Josef, you would have been proud of him. He kept them off his land, and he fought to keep the war out of our little community," she replied. "The thugs. That's all they were."

"Thugs," Josef repeated.

"I must tell Kurt how his father died."

"We'll tell him together after this is all over." They held each other close. "I worry for Kurt after the war is over and the Americans and Russians have won."

The small room became quiet as the bombardment diminished in its intensity. Josef heard Maria's slow steady breathing as she lay next to him. He knew the hours had passed and he suspected morning was not far away. He rose, dressed, and tip-toed from the room, closing the squeaky door behind him.

He slowly came down the many stairs deep in thought. *If all is lost, what do we do?* He thought with growing anxiety. *My beautiful wife… What will become of her? I cannot allow the murderous bastards to harm her.*

Josef had to prepare for the battle that was coming to Castle Itter.

CHAPTER 17

May 5, 1945, 0430 hours

Major Gangl entered the great hall and quickly located Captain Lee, who was quietly sitting in a chair smoking a cigar. His eyes closed, he seemed to be thinking. Several of his men were also awake. They were boiling water for coffee and examining weapons and ammo. Two Wehrmacht soldiers of Major Gangl, on the opposite side of the large room, were sipping water and dressing. They talked among themselves. Everyone smoked.

Jack opened his eyes to see the Austrian approach. "Major, good of you to join us."

"Captain, it will be daylight soon. I will inspect the men," Josef said.

"I should assist you, Major," he replied. Standing, he grabbed his cartridge belt to buckle it around him. The two men climbed the steps. The two Austrian Wehrmacht and three American soldiers watched them mount the stairs. The two former enemies of just a few days earlier now together inspected positions. Both seemed uncomfortable in their new roles, as were their men. Surprisingly, there were no confrontations or even disagreements.

"Strange," Josef remarked. "Today, we will fight the German SS, and all will pray the American Army arrives before it is too late."

Fog hugged the tree line in the early morning darkness. The dense cloud cover almost touched the ground. Both men knew that would prevent any air support from reaching them before the fighting began. Standing on the ramparts high above the mostly open ground in front, the two officers tried to extrapolate where the infantry would advance. They both realized there was only one direction that allowed any type of advance to threaten the castle walls, and that was the front gate that faced the road.

"I have placed all my sharpshooters here, here, and over there," Jack said, pointing to the different positions where the GIs lay about, some sleeping while others were on lookout. He looked at the major. "I hope you're not offended but I've taken charge in your absence last night."

"Captain, I defer to you," Josef said, somehow feeling relieved he would not give the orders to kill his former comrades in arms. "For my men and me, it is better that way, I think."

They walked the ramparts, assigning positions to the five men who were with them. When they passed American soldiers, Jack introduced them to Josef, and the same when passing Josef's men.

Josef thought morale was high considering they were vastly outnumbered and outgunned. They laughed and joked with the men even though most of their stories were lost in translation. Reaching the gate, they looked down on the bridge and the lone Sherman tank. Here they placed the remainder of their men. They placed the single machine gun above the arch for maximum effect. They knew they had to hold the bridge, or the fight was over.

"Are there many rounds inside your tank, Captain?"

"Full up," Jack replied. "We'll shoot them all right down the damn road." Josef liked the sound of that. "That should slow them down."

"Yeah, but soon as they get their sights on her, that's it." "You plan to pull her back off the bridge?"

"Hell no! She stays right there."

Josef smiled. "Good, good," he replied. They both turned to return to the main hall.

They came down the stairs as Maria entered. Josef saw immediately that she wore her gun belt and was prepared to do battle.

Their world was still shrouded in darkness, as the hour was early. "Maria," Josef called to her. "Wake everyone and get ready." "They must eat, but we have no more."

"We can fix that," Jack said. "Corporal, gather up all the C-rations and bring them inside."

"Yessir," he replied and left.

Paul Reynaud, the only French prisoner in the hall, watched. He had found a German pistol and ammo and had stuffed it in his belt. Jack and Josef saw the weapon, and both appreciated that everyone was preparing for the fight.

Another American soldier brought tins of coffee. "Get the water boiling. I have coffee—real American coffee—for everyone."

The corporal and another soldier carried in boxes of C-rations. "We have enough food for everyone if you don't mind army rations."

"Those would be a feast compared to what we've been eating the last several years," Reynaud said.

"And I cook 'em like the best chefs in Paris," the corporal said proudly. Reynaud nodded but very much doubted the young man's assertion.

Maria looked at the soldier opening the box of rations with a knife. "Ja, da, thank you," she said, her English limited.

Soon, several small fires burned in the hall as the Americans turned their c-ration cans into small hot plates to boil coffee.

Maria stared out the long narrow window through the courtyard at the lone American tank sitting on the bridge. The crew gathered behind it in the darkness. They smoked cigarettes cupped in their palms, not wanting to draw sniper fire. In the darkness, she heard noise, a rumbling of engines. The mortar fire resumed with added intensity. Shadows danced among the trees.

The tank crew waited nervously for their orders.

They are taking positions, Maria thought. The battle is soon.

While inside, the aroma of coffee drifted through the air. Jack went over the plan with his NCOs. Everyone present soon sipped coffee.

The other prisoners began to gather around the table as they had done hundreds of times during their imprisonment. Josef saw immediately that they needed to be briefed and armed. "Maria, where are the weapons?" he asked.

"We have stacked them in the corner with ammunition."

"Please have someone distribute them," he replied. "Daylight is soon, and we can expect the attack. When they are armed, I will place them in position."

Maria smiled and nodded. It felt good hearing his voice, but she was not used to him giving her orders. After the ordeal with the Gestapo and her experiences at Dachau and with Captain Wimmer, she wondered if she would obey anyone ever again. "I will feed them, Josef," she said, assertive.

Reynaud watched her work. He liked her strength, intelligence, and leadership abilities. "Are you ready to assist me, young lady?" he asked.

"First I eat," she replied.

"Yes, yes, of course," Reynaud replied.

"We eat then kill Krauts," the American corporal added. Everyone turned to look at the soldier.

"Whoops, sorry," he said.

The Americans laid food, all C-rations and A-rations they had brought with them, on the long table, and immediately, soldiers, prisoners, and inmates were at the table grabbing. Everyone took a ration and quickly returned to their fighting position.

Kurt entered from the courtyard where he had been preparing defenses. He was taken aback. The gathering around the table surprised him. The sight of Americans, French, and Austrians eating together amicably was uncomfortable for him.

"What is this?" he demanded in a raised voice.

The former prisoners looked at their former captor, and then ignored him. The Americans watched him with suspicion.

"Kurt, the Americans have brought food for us. Eat," Maria told him sternly. "I will not." He looked contemptuously first at the cans of food and then at the American soldiers.

His behavior was noticed by everyone, but especially by the Americans. "Hey!"

Eat, ya Kraut bastard," the corporal in charge of preparations scolded. "Kurt, please," Maria said.

Scowling, he looked at her, and without much pleasure, grabbed a cup of coffee and a box of rations. "Go to hell," he growled under his breath. Maria heard.

"They are here to help us, to fight for us. Please… " she chastised him. Without speaking, he headed for the staircase, a C-ration tucked under his arm.

Explosions from mortar rounds grew more intense, driving everyone outside down to avoid shrapnel. Major Gangl and Captain Lee together observed the open area directly in front of the castle where they knew the battle would be waged.

"Your wife, eh?" Jack asked, still looking out the window. "A very beautiful woman, and strong, too."

Josef turned to look at the American. "She is, and she has her own mind. We've known each other since childhood, and she has always been strong-willed."

"Strong-willed… yes." Jack smiled, thinking of his wife. "My wife, too." "Soon," Josef said. "Are your sharpshooters in position?"

"Yup," Jack replied. "Best shots in the division."

Josef nodded without looking at the American. "Our success may depend on that." He turned to visit his men around the gate, greeting and offering encouragement to each man.

Jack turned to leave him. "I must get a better view. The sun is breaking, giving us more light," he said.

Josef agreed and accompanied him again as they ran through the main hall and up the staircase. On the ramparts, they tried to get a panoramic view of the tree line and meadow in front.

They continued observing and watched for signs of any SS advance from the trees. They saw the Sherman alone on the bridge guarding them like a well-trained shepherd.

"I think I can buy us a little more time," Jack announced, an urgent thought flashing in his mind. He turned and ran back down the long staircase. Josef watched, amused, as he raced through the courtyard to stop beside the tank crew cowering in the stone gate just behind the tank.

Suddenly, a sharpshooter fired into the forest. "I see movement," the shooter called to Josef.

Josef bent down beside the shooter to have a closer look. He saw nothing, but he knew they were there awaiting their orders.

"Get ready," he said loudly so everyone would hear. Everyone on the ramparts raised their weapons and prepared for the attack.

Back in the courtyard, Jack greeted his tank commander. Josef watched from above as Jack pointed at the sun. The commander seemed to understand. That was the order they waited on. "Shoot every round if you can. Aim the gun right down the damn road," Jack called to them. "We have to keep those big Tigers from getting out and forming up in the clearing. When you've fired everything, get the hell out of there. Leave her sitting on top the bridge. Get back here. Is that understood?"

"Got it. Run like hell," the commander replied. Two tankers ran for their Sherman and jumped atop it, then disappeared inside.

Soon, the turret lowered and pointed down the narrow road that led through the trees.

Josef saw movement.

The tank's single machine gun opened up, spraying lead across the tree line. Suddenly, Besotten Jenny's big gun growled loudly, firing a round directly down the road. It continued firing as fast as the experienced gunner could load and extract shells. The tank jumped with each round.

Josef smiled, feeling reassured his American allies were getting into the fight.

He turned to return to the lowest level and join Lee.

Small arms fire from the trees zinged overhead or bounced harmlessly off the massive stone walls.

Jack looked closely into the trees while the sharpshooters opened up all along the castle wall. He saw the enemy moving forward, but still in the tree line. He saw men fall in the dim but growing light, hit by his sharpshooters. Others stepped forward to take their place firing at his men as they moved forward in a line, but still using the trees as cover.

He spit, threw his butt onto the stone, and turned to run across the courtyard for the main door.

Major Gangl, having just returned from the high walls, greeted him. "Tell your men at the gate to conserve ammo, get good targets. We're short," he said.

"Right," Jack nodded.

The sun crept above the forest. Shadows danced in front of the trees. The enemy waited for the order to move forward. They heard German Tigers lumbering down the road to reach the clearing despite the constant firing of the smaller gun of the American Sherman.

The noise was almost deafening. Maria put her hands to her ears to block it out but was unsuccessful. She had never been exposed to anything like this. Seeing Josef, she ran to him.

"It has started," she said. "The noise. It's deafening." "Yes, the battle has started," he replied.

"How will it end?"

Josef looked at her with almost five years of combat experience behind him but said nothing.

She knew he would not answer her question. "The last hours having you here with me have been wonderful," she said. "Whatever happens, I will cherish these memories forever."

He said nothing but held her close.

CHAPTER 18

Jack, peering from the large window, saw a large dark object in the shadows moving toward them. It seemed to be coming down the road and straight at them like an angry bull charging into the open meadow. "Major, look. What do you see?"

"A tank. Tiger. The infantry won't leave their cover until at least one of their tanks is positioned in the clearing. The road is narrow. The tanks must move down single file, and that is giving us more time."

"More time for what, Major?" Jack asked. Josef smiled. "For a miracle to happen."

"Gather around," Jack called to those inside the great hall. "Sergeant Glenn," he said to his ranking NCO in the castle. "Round up the Frenchies. One last order."

"Yes sir."

Meanwhile, the Sherman continued firing, throwing shell after shell on and around the road. Seeing the German tank enter the clearing moving to its left, the gun shifted, pointing its barrel directly at the massive steel hulk moving across their field of vision.

The first round nailed the tank but bounced off the corner of the frontal steel. They fired a second as the tank continued moving across the open area to get into position. This time the round hit the turret, killing its commander instantly. The Tiger ground to a halt, smoke rising from a fire inside. Soon, the crew who survived the blast bailed out.

The commander of the Sherman watched jubilantly, but knew it was too early to celebrate. The second Tiger entered the clearing with a great growl, determined to inflict revenge on the Americans. It moved menacingly toward the Sherman.

The remainder of the tank's crew behind the stone gate yelled to the men inside their tank. "Get out! Now! Hey Sarge, it's coming at you."

Inside, with Josef still standing beside him to translate if necessary, Jack quickly explained what he needed. "All women. Position yourselves at the windows, stay low, and prepare to fire at any man wearing a camouflage uniform who enters the courtyard. I want the men to join the soldiers near the gate. If we must retreat, I want the Czech to open the door for us. Where's the Czech?" He looked around to find Cuckovic. "Major, tell him what I want."

Locating him among the servants, Josef with Prusha explained in Czech but mostly in German what he expected of him. Cuckovic nodded that he understood.

"Also, I want you to assist one of my boys here with getting the wounded inside." Prusha translated, and Cuckovic seemed to understand.

Everyone heard the constant tank fire outside. Lee and Gangl easily distinguished between the German and American guns. Jack was relieved it was mostly his boys firing, but he knew the Tigers would begin heavier firing immediately. So far, their rounds were pounding the castle walls but with little effect. They would soon focus on the gate and the Sherman in front, and he knew the time to get the boys out of the Sherman was almost there.

Maria approached Josef. "I will not be told what is expected of me," she said, looking at Jack. "I will go outside and fight beside the men. If you are at the gate, I, too, will be there."

She caught both men by surprise.

Jack looked at her with her weapon and smiled. "You do whatever you've decided to do," he said, not interested in handling an insurrection now that the battle had begun.

"No, you will stay here and fight from the window. I insist," Josef said, both frustrated and frightened for her safety. "It is too dangerous, and you have only a pistol."

"I am going, husband. We will fight together and die together if that fate befalls us."

Paul Reynaud stepped forward to place himself between the two. "Major, I will ask that you allow me to voice an opinion." He looked at both husband and wife. "Maria?"

Maria and Josef, surprised by the interference, looked at the Frenchman. "Speak monsieur, what is it?" Josef asked sharply with growing anger... and fear for his wife.

"These many days I have come to know your wife well and have learned to respect her abilities and insight," the Frenchman continued.

"Da?" Josef replied with growing impatience.

Jack stepped back to allow the three to resolve problems he considered a disagreement between husband and wife.

"Major, since your wife has excellent observation and reasoning skills, I request that she be assigned to me. As I have agreed to Captain Lee's request that I supervise the fighting on the roof, I believe she would offer excellent assistance as my, how do you say, assistant, aide-de-camp. She will work with me. Is that agreeable?"

Josef stared at the Frenchman with mounting anger. "Monsieur Reynaud, I would greatly appreciate it if you... "

"I accept, Paul," Maria interjected. "I would be honored to serve as your assistant."

"Excellent," Jack said. "To the ramparts. Everyone, go to your battle stations," he ordered loud enough for everyone to hear.

Josef, still angry and frustrated, did not move. Maria saw this. "Please Josef, we have all given enough in this horrid place, and should be allowed to make our own decisions if we want. You are my husband, and it is important to me that you accept it."

Josef said nothing but turned to leave with the American captain.

Everyone deployed except the fascists who stayed sitting at the long table. They seemed indifferent to what was happening around them.

Both the American and Reynaud noticed.

Reynaud, with Maria, walked to the table to stand in front of them. "Get up," he ordered.

Neither moved.

"I order you to stand," he repeated.

At first, they did not move but both smiled broadly to mock the former premier of France. Two American soldiers who saw what was happening approached with rifles.

"You will assist us in this fight or face a firing squad. It is your choice."

"We'll shoot them now and save you the trouble," one of the GIs replied, the sound of his voice cold and determined.

The fascists—La Rocque and Poncet—stood slowly, carefully watching the two Americans, with their M-1s pointed at their chests. Looks of panic etched their features. From the M-1s or having to return to the arch was unknown.

"You heard, so the choice is yours," Reynaud said. He was pleased to get the support of the young Americans with the help of their rifles.

The two immediately jumped up from their chairs and left to assist the others preparing to do battle.

"Ammo carriers," Renaud called to the others in English. "They will carry ammo for us up the stairs." He pointed at the two Fascists.

The Americans gave him a thumbs-up in reply.

Jack rushed outside, through the courtyard to the stone arch. It was time to get them out of the tank. He watched the Tiger position itself to fire point-blank at the Sherman.

"Hey, get out!" he called. Men around him, seeing him calling, also began to yell at the two men inside the Sherman.

"Get out!" Everyone yelled.

CHAPTER 19

Joaquin Speers directed his men and their machines as they slowly entered the meadow from the tree-lined road. The last tank was still on the road. Everything was moving too slow, he thought. "Go! Go!" he yelled to urge more speed. "Their bullets can't stop our tanks."

He stood on the road behind the last tank. Looking through binoculars, he watched the castle gate and the American tank parked on the bridge. Its gun barrel had sighted and was firing directly on the first two tanks. He knew the American tank would become an easy target for his larger, more powerful Tigers once they sighted in and began to fire. The lighter armored Sherman could not withstand the heavier Tigers with their much bigger guns.

His aide stood silently beside him, their vehicle behind them parked along the road. "A shame that they decided to make a fight of it," he softly said to the young lieutenant. "Now, many men will die. Why? Why Lieutenant?" he asked rhetorically. "To save the French losers and the other scum of Europe? They should have been shot already. Now my men and the Americans must fight and die."

"Sir?"

Speers sighed and lowered his binoculars. He turned to the young man. "But it is war, and that is what soldiers must do, eh Lieutenant?"

"I am prepared to fight, Major."

"Yes, I believe you are." Speers gave his aide a steady, unblinking look. He suddenly doubted very much if this young naive man was really prepared to fight and die. He had joined the battalion after the fighting around Vienna, and not during the long retreat from Kursk. He had not experienced enough to know his own worth. Speers suspected he had joined the battalion mostly to escape the Russian advance into Germany, and capture or worse, death at the hands of the barbaric Asiatics.

Everyone heard explosions from tank fire coming from the village of Worgl. Speers recognized the gun—a Sherman. He had to establish some type of defensive line to hold them. The battle for Castle Itter grew more intense. The SS soldiers responded to the sniper fire with machine gun fire. They pounded positions at the gate and along the ramparts. A line of infantry suddenly moved out of the trees to assault the American tank and bridge. Both attackers and defenders knew the battle would hinge on their success.

Small arms fire from the castle walls increased with the defenders pouring bullets into the German line. Those poor fools will run out of ammo soon, Speers hoped.

A messenger reported that the Americans hit the first tank with heavy fire and knocked it out. "Sir, they hit the turret with a lucky shot," he said.

Speers was concerned. The American tank's relentless firing slowed their advance to barely a crawl, and casualties were mounting. He paced around the staff car, growing more anxious. He knew the remainder of the American armor units could not be too far away. He looked up at the sky, still overcast. He seemed relieved. "At least they're getting no air support," he said to his aide. But that could quickly change, he knew.

"We must move faster and take it before the rest of the Americans arrive," he said.

"Sir, casualties," the young man replied. "The Americans on the walls are very good shots, I think."

"We must move faster, hit them harder. Those walls can take only so much pounding before they collapse. Target the gate."

"Ja, sir."

"Send the order to the commanders and to the infantry, too."

"Right away, Herr Major," he replied. He prepared to leave, but suddenly looked up. "I hear airplanes above the clouds. They will strike when the fog lifts. How do we fight them? We have no airplanes or antiaircraft guns."

Speers looked hard at his aide. "We must take it before the fog lifts, Lieutenant."

The aide did not reply, but he did not leave.

"We must take the castle quickly. It is our only hope, or they will wipe us out. Time is of the essence. Tell the men that. Urgent. Do you understand that?" Speers said, stress seeping into his words, but he knew it was his own anxiety. His men were doing all they could.

"Ja, sir." He ran off toward the front to pass the word to all officers and NCOs.

He decided he could no longer stay in the woods. He had to get closer to the fight and take charge himself. Braving bullets whizzing over his head, he marched down the road toward his men. He reached the last tank as it entered the open meadow.

"Get behind the tanks," he ordered. A bullet grazed his shoulder, throwing him off balance. He slumped against the tank.

Seeing his commander take a hit, the young lieutenant ran to him. He helped him stand, and the two of them ran to the cover of the trees, but his infantry obeyed. They ran to the left to use the tanks' cover. The machine gunners remained under cover of the trees, firing round after round at the sharpshooters atop the ramparts.

The rifle fire from the high points was devastating, he saw. They positioned their snipers well, he thought, impressed. But Speers knew, like the defenders, that the shooters could slow but not halt their steady advance across the meadow into the Castle grounds.

CHAPTER 20

The two men inside Besotten Jenny also knew it was time to get out. They watched as the big German tank prepared to fire its gun directly at them, and at this range, it would destroy the smaller Sherman. Their ammo was running low, and they had done all they could to slow the SS advance. For the tank commander, the decision was easy. "Corporal, let's get the hell out of here."

"Got it. I'll open the hatch. Then run for it." He forced it open. Bullets dinged against it.

They heard yelling from the gate. The time to escape was now.

"Go," the commander ordered. The gunner poked his head through, and then lifting the rest of his body, he rolled off the back of the tank and ran for the gate. The commander immediately followed.

Suddenly, a deafening explosion threw rocks and steel in all directions as a round struck the bridge beside the Sherman. The third Tiger had fired from the road, but still emerging from the woods, attempting for a better advantage.

A piece of steel hit the American in the back as he jumped from the rear of the tank. The concussion blew him to the ground. Still alive, he tried with all his might to stand, but fell again. Blood darkened his shirt, trousers, and ran from his nose.

The gunner, seeing him lying there but still alive, ran to rescue him. Under withering machine gun fire from German tanks, he grabbed his sergeant, threw him onto his shoulder and ran like hell back under the gate.

"Hey Leroy," another American called to the gunner. "How is he?" "He'll live," Leroy replied. "They got our range, so watch out."

The Tiger fired again, its big gun rocking the tank. The round smashed against the Sherman. The American tank burst into flame but did not move from the bridge.

"Glad to be out of there," Leroy said. "Help me get him into the castle." The two men took the wounded tank commander and dragged him across the courtyard and into the main hall. They heard another loud noise as the other tank in the clearing fired. This round hit the stone wall, but the wall held with only steel and bits of stone flung into the air.

Jack observed the German infantry bringing up a .88 MM howitzer, and he knew that they were determined to move Besotten Jenny out of the way. "Get back!" he ordered everyone.

The .88 fired. Its round struck the American tank head on. The explosion ignited fuel and unspent ammunition still inside the already destroyed Sherman, but what remained of the steel hulk held its position on the bridge.

"Hey, get the .88," Jack called up to his sharpshooters. "The damn .88!" He pointed.

More German infantry emerged from the trees to follow behind the remaining tanks, firing as they moved forward. All movement converged on the bridge. They fired at the gate and into the courtyard.

The defenders below cowered behind the heavy stone prepared for the howitzer to fire again. Above, Lee's sharpshooters continued to do their job, trying to pin the Germans down with accurate shooting into their ranks. Now trying to silence the .88, they fired round after round at both howitzer's crewmembers. Finally, both Germans fell to the ground and the gun went quiet.

At least temporarily stopped, Jack thought, pleased with the good shooting. The Americans, Wehrmacht, and partisans quickly returned to their firing positions and opened up on the SS infantry trying to sweep toward the gate. Men on both sides fell. The tanks moved forward, inching closer to the Sherman, still guarding the entrance like St. Peter at the pearly gates. Their infantry began to cluster tightly behind the Tigers, which limited their ability to pour heavy fire on their targets.

"Spread out," Speers ordered from the behind the last tank with growing concern.

Both Lee and Gangl shouted encouragement to their men as they ran heads down along the walled courtyard. Bullets flew everywhere around them, but most struck the thick stone walls. They heard yelling from high above, and fearing trouble, looked up.

"I'm going up to the ramparts," Josef shouted. "Got to hold this gate." "Gotcha," Jack replied.

When Josef arrived on top, Kurt joined him.

Men around them fell, mostly from flying bits of stone. The intensity of the incoming fire forced them to hug the narrow walkway. Josef saw that ammo was running low.

"We cannot hold out up here much longer, Major," a sharpshooter called to Josef.

"Josef, the tank. We got to stop it," Kurt yelled, interrupting.

"It will not get by the American tank," Josef replied above the gunfire. "Where is Maria?" He quickly searched the wall with his eyes.

"She is with the Frenchman. I think they are attending the wounded."

"Keep up the fire on the infantry. They are nearing the gate. I will send up more ammo," he replied calmly. "We must hold the gate at all costs," he repeated.

"We will hold," Kurt replied with renewed fortitude.

"I must find my wife," Josef said, and ran downstairs to return to the great hall.

Kurt understood, grabbed a rifle from one of the incapacitated wounded and began to fire down at his former comrades. Well aware that his life depended on it, he did so without hesitation.

Jack and Maria were with the wounded including the tank commander just brought in. The other wounded lying on the floor were hit on the ramparts. The heavy fighting outside muted their moans.

"You doing okay, Sarge?" Jack asked above the noise.

"Yeah, got knocked a little silly, but should be ready for more in a couple of minutes."

"You did an excellent job," Jack replied, patting him on the shoulder. He brought out a fresh cigar, clipped the end with his pocketknife, and plopped it in his mouth. He prepared to light up, then looked at Maria.

"Here?" Maria asked, frowning at him. "Among the wounded?"

"I guess not." He blew out the match. "I'll go out front to the gate. Sounds like they're getting close and need my help."

"Be careful," Maria said. She looked up to see Josef charging down the stairs.

She smiled.

Jack looked at her, amused.

"Maria," Josef said. "I had to find you." He looked around, and seeing no one nearby, kissed her.

She touched his face. "These men... We have limited medical supplies, mostly from the Americans. All I can do is stop the bleeding, comfort them, and give them water."

"You're doing your best," Josef replied.

"Damn right she is," the tank commander added. "A great woman ya got there."

"She's the best," Josef said. "Where is the Frenchman, Reynaud?" "He is over there near the window. Why?"

"We need more ammo upstairs."

"He will find someone to do it," Maria said, focusing on her work assisting with the wounded.

"Paul, more ammo on the ramparts. Where is it?" he asked, calling above the rifle fire and explosions outside the hall.

Reynaud paused to look around before answering. He had just returned from the ramparts. "What we have is over there." He pointed to the corner. He looked for the two Fascists appointed as ammo humpers but did not see them. "Bridget, take the .30 caliber ammunition up and hurry," he called to the young woman. "They can do more damage up there."

Without a word, she ran to the corner, grabbed as many boxes as she could carry, and with the extra weight of ammo, struggled up the stairs.

"Good," Josef said. He looked around to ensure everyone was at their window posts. He found the two Fascists cowering in the corner near a single window. One of them was armed with a pistol. He hoped they would fight the invaders when they had to. They must know that they will not be spared either, he thought.

Knowing the American captain was under the arch, Josef decided to return to the ramparts to direct operations. He ran back up the wide staircase.

Maria watched him. "Paul I'm going up," she called to Reynaud. "There's nothing more I can do here for the moment.

"I will accompany you." He grabbed a rifle lying unclaimed on the floor and ran to catch up. It was a Mauser. "More targets there," he said to no one as he took the steps two at a time.

Jack made his way to the arched gate with bullets growling at his ears. The engine noise from the Tigers rose above the sound of rifle and machine gun fire. The last tank moved along the tree line for a position to the left of the second. Both drove toward the bridge. Each stopped to fire at the stone walls, then moved forward again, creeping toward the defenders. Bits of stone and steel flew in all directions, but the wall did not collapse.

Jack looked up at their only machine gun. It was still active, firing round after round at the men massing below. He saw Captain Schrader operating it with one of his boys feeding the belt of ammo. The other man—an American—lay beside his buddy on the rampart unconscious, blood draining from his body.

Goddammit, he cursed to himself. The loss of even one of his boys was hard for him to bear. After months together, he knew all of them. They were his family.

Their small arms fire at the German advance continued its intensity. Yet, the enemy inched their way closer behind the tank despite their growing casualties.

"Assault the gate," Speers called to his men. "Now!" His men, however, looked confused and disorganized.

"Captain," Speers called to an officer in front of him. "Organize your men.

Can't you see? They're running low on ammo at the gate. The time is now."

Above, Gangl worked his way around the ramparts to the arch where Schrader was on the American gun. He heard someone calling him, turned. It was Maria.

She ran toward him. "Josef! Josef!" she called. "What is it?"

"I had to tell you I love you. Something... I love you," she said, from behind the wall. There they embraced and held each other tight if only for a second with Reynaud looking on. Both understood that time was running out. In their hearts, they knew...

"We've brought more ammo and an additional rifle," Reynaud said, laying down the boxes then sorting them out. This one is for the American weapons and this one for the German." The Mauser went unclaimed, so he kneeled behind the wall and began firing it.

"Good, good. Maria, divide it among them," Josef told her. He pointed to the two Americans and one Austrian who remained on the wall. "I must help Kurt. He's on the arch." He kissed her, turned, and ran low toward the front arch.

On the stairway, Bridget greeted Maria as she returned to the hall for more ammo. Bridget looked hard at Maria, appearing deeply concerned.

"What is it?" Maria asked.

"We're almost out of ammunition. We cannot bring any more up. Everything now is for those at the gate."

In the main hall, Maria took charge without hesitation. "Where is Jean?" she asked Bridget.

"Outside. He ran out to the gate. I just saw him," Bridget replied.

"With ammunition?"

"Yes, I think," she said. "His arms were full." "We must have more for the German guns. Any?"

Everyone looked around them. "We have only what each of us needs," Marie Cailliau replied.

"You," she called to the Fascists. "Come here. Now!"

The two men looked at her warily. They thought they had found a safe place. "Give up your pistols," Maria ordered the two fascists—La Rocque and Poncet.

"I will give them to a hero. I'm placing you both on medical detail. You will retrieve the wounded from the gate."

"No, please," Poncet replied, a look of terror etching his features. He knew the fighting outside had only grown worse and more desperate.

"Go or I will shoot you where you stand," Maria said, collecting their weapons. Bridget smiled, enjoying Maria's rough treatment of the two.

"We must make every round count," she said to others nearby. "When the soldiers charge through the gate everyone must shoot. We cannot afford to waste any ammunition. Every bullet must count."

Josef joined the fight above the arch. The Germans were focusing all their efforts on breaking through and the only way in was across the bridge. He could see that they were massing behind the forward tank for an assault after the first attempt failed to break through to the courtyard.

"Throw everything at them, boys," Jack said, and began to fire his .45 from underneath the arch. They watched as the second Tiger attempted to push the Sherman's smoking ruins off the bridge and into the moat. "There," Jack yelled, pointing at a vulnerable spot in the armor. The GI fired his tanker's submachine gun across the turret hoping to hit someone, but the .45 caliber bullets bounced off the steel, hitting no one.

"Panzerfaust! Bring it up," Josef, standing above the gate, called to one of his men.

The frontal plate of the heavy Tiger smashed into the front of the Sherman, attempting to drive the smaller, lighter tank off the bridge into the moat. It failed. The tank moved but only inches.

"Panzerfaust! Hurry!" Josef repeated with increased concern.

The Americans, not understanding, looked at each other and then at Major Gangl, as a Wehrmacht soldier ran across the ramparts for the weapon. He returned quickly and positioned himself by kneeling down on top of the arch with the antitank weapon. He aimed the weapon from his shoulder while another man inserted the round in the tube.

"Fire it at the first tank," Schrader ordered. "We must stop it." The man aimed at the tank's track, knowing the Tiger was vulnerable there.

"Fire!" Kurt yelled.

Thump! The rocket flew directly at the Tiger. It struck the tank at an angle, smashing into the right track. The explosion threw hot bits of steel into the air. The tank growled angrily but could not move forward.

Having stopped the large machine from pushing the Sherman off the bridge, they successfully blocked movement of any machine across the bridge.

Josef and Kurt knew that improved their odds of survival. Still heavily outnumbered, but the SS infantry, lacking direct support from their armor, would now pay dearly to get into the courtyard and beyond. Infantry verses infantry. I like that, Josef thought, knowing that evened the odds ever slightly.

They immobilized the heavy tank, but they failed to knock it out. Its larger gun turned and lowered to find its next target, while its machine gunner still hammered away at targets around the gate.

"Get another rocket before it fires again," Kurt called to the soldier beside him. "The turret. We must knock out the turret."

The man reacted quickly but not fast enough. The big gun found its target.

Seeing the gun raise to their level, both Kurt and Josef yelled. "Get off the bridge. Take the weapons and get off."

Austrians, Americans, and French scattered in all directions. Several jumped off the ten feet high arch to the courtyard below.

The Tiger gun exploded just as they scattered. The round hit the stone arch sending tremors out across the stone. Its machine gun opened up with a burst aimed at the defenders beneath the arch. The tank crew attempted to give their soldiers an opportunity to charge the opening.

Jack looked up at the sun fighting to break through the cloud cover. How long yet? he wondered. If he could just get some air support, he knew the tide of battle would quickly turn in their favor. He pointed up at the sky. "Soon," he said to everyone standing near him. He was supremely confident American airpower would not let him down. They could be depended on to save the day, as they had so many times during the past months. He prayed now was no different.

The German infantry again attempted to break through the gate, but they ran into obstacles they had created. With debris partially blocking access across the narrow bridge and under the arch, they were forced to change tactics. They began to move from tank to tank. Soon too many clustered behind the burned-out American tank, joining survivors of earlier assaults. Because of the continued heavy fire from the defenders, they were trapped. The deadly incoming from above forced them to stay down for cover.

The Tiger fired again. Its 40 mm round struck the 800-year-old stone structure with a great blast, leaving it shattered. Bits of stone flew in all directions. The arch did not collapse, but the blast from the tank caught the Panzerfaust team as they tried to retreat behind the heavy stone. One member of the two-man team fell, hit by shrapnel. He lay seriously wounded, but the other man made it to cover. Machine gun bullets from the tank stitched the entire span of bridge.

"Get that gun," Josef called to Kurt. From higher on the wall, rifle shots rang out but bounced off the steel.

Kurt grabbed the German bazooka. "Gimme that round." The surviving member of the team loaded it into the weapon. Kurt stepped out into the open. He aimed it at the turret of the tank and fired.

A direct hit. The turret erupted in fire and the machine gun grew silent. "Good shot," Josef yelled. He looked around the ramparts. "We got to get the wounded out. Boys take them back along the ramparts but stay low. Hurry."

The third tank, forced to halt in the open field well behind the damaged tank, fired its main gun to continue the barrage focused on the arch.

A .30 caliber round hit a GI as he attempted to drag a wounded man back. He lay on the rubble, bleeding but alive. "Help me," he moaned, lying in the open on top of the arch.

Major Gangl ran out from the ramparts to rescue the wounded man while others drug the other man to safety. He grabbed him by the arms and began to move him back under cover.

The big gun fired again.

A round again struck the stone just above the arch, exploding to send shrapnel in all directions. The ancient stone shook violently, deep fissures suddenly pulsating through the mortar, and finally collapsed. The arch was no more. Heavy stone and wood debris rained down on the defenders. The powerful explosion sent both Josef and the wounded American flying into the air, bloodied by multiple bits of hot steel punching into their bodies. They fell to the courtyard, buried under the rubble.

Seeing the advantage offered by their tanks, German rifle fire increased its intensity. "Attack," Speers ordered from behind the third tank. He knew the time was now.

With the defenders thrown into disarray by the big guns, the SS soldiers charged the gate while others took their position behind the forward tanks to support them.

"Get back, get back to your positions," Captain Lee screamed. Those who could, obeyed and returned to the gate, firing as they ran. They met the oncoming Germans. Fighting at close quarters among the stone was ferocious. Finally, the defenders succeeded in driving back the assault. Casualties on both sides were surprisingly light, but the ammo situation was acute.

Jack saw that his men were becoming fewer, that their ammo was running low. They continued to fire at the attackers, but he knew they would soon be overwhelmed. "Pull back! Get the wounded and pull back," he ordered. He sensed the end of the battle was near. Out-gunned and out-manned, the SS was quickly gaining the upper hand.

His small combined force threw everything they had at the enemy, but they now had to withdraw. They retreated quickly across the courtyard. Heavy stone from the collapsed arch protected their retreat, giving them time to offer covering fire.

The enemy tanks halted their fire, unable to distinguish friend from foe in the melee inside the courtyard. Meeting less resistance, Speers ordered more men through the destroyed gate. Large stones strewn across their path slowed their advance and gave the defenders time to escape inside the castle.

Looking up as he retreated, Jack searched for Major Gangl, but could not find him in the smoke and dust. He waved to those on the front ramparts above. Locating Captain Schrader in the chaos and confusion behind the ramparts, he yelled, "Cover us."

Hearing the American, Kurt and the dwindling number of Americans and Austrians still with him fired down on the attackers until their comrades had cleared the area. Finally, with his ammo gone, visibility limited to only several feet, Jack had no choice but to pull back with his men behind the walls of the great hall.

Josef lay mortally wounded on the walk facing the courtyard alongside the American soldier he tried to save. Stone and dust partially covered their bodies.

The defenders who had been at the gate with their commander rushed through the door into the main hall. Jack followed last to ensure everyone got in. Many carried and dragged wounded with them.

"Bridget, go up and bring everyone from the ramparts down," Jack ordered.

He slammed the double doors behind him.

The young woman raced up the stairs and returned immediately. Reynaud had remained on top to ensure all the men including the wounded retreated to the man hall.

Maria stood at the window nearest the double door firing at the invaders. "Where's Josef? Where is my husband?" she asked loudly but not in a panic… yet. She ran to Jack still by the entrance door. "Where is Major Gangl?" she asked him. "I demand that you tell me where my husband is."

Jack looked at her, appearing to form his words carefully. "Out there. He was killed in the last tank blast. I'm sorry. There was nothing I could do."

Maria was silent.

"He tried to save one of my men and was blown off the arch. I'm sorry," he repeated. "He lay in the stone debris beside the man he tried to save. I looked but could not find him."

"I will find him," she replied resolutely. "I will bring him in." She stepped to the door prepared to open it, gun still drawn, but the incoming fire was so intense that it forced everyone to the floor. Bullets hammered the walls. Those at the windows dropped to the floor as mostly small arms fire from the arch peppered the sills and interior walls. The glass had already been broken out in preparation for the expected assault.

"Stay down," Jack ordered everyone.

The firing continued but gradually slowed to sporadic, which told Jack that the Germans had to conserve their ammo, too.

"To your firing positions at the windows. We must stop them here!" he screamed. He then helped move the wounded to the far side of the room to get them out of the way. "How many grenades do we have, Krouse?" he asked the German sergeant.

He understood what the American wanted. "I will find them, Herr Captain," he replied.

Two American soldiers joined Maria at the window. Unused to fighting beside a woman, they tried to shield her from the incoming bullets, but she wound have none of it. "I want to kill every one of the bastards," she said in English to the Americans.

They looked at her surprised, but they understood how she felt.

Sergeant Krouse searched through the room for grenades. "Five or six, Captain," he announced when he returned seconds later. He deposited them on the floor at their feet.

They were German 'potato smashers.'

"Get the American grenades, too," Jack ordered.

Krouse obeyed, returning with four American 'pineapples.' "That'll have to hold them off."

Seconds passed quickly. Bullets continued to pepper the walls, coming through the windows as the SS soldiers outside consolidated their position. Mortar rounds fell mostly in the courtyard, harmlessly throwing up dirt. It was obvious to everyone inside that the enemy was preparing for a final assault. "Hold back on the grenades until they are in the middle of the courtyard," Jack ordered.

He moved around the large room talking with the former POWs, congregated on the facing wall, with their weapons and dwindling supplies of ammo beside them. Everyone waited and prayed silently. "Find a target, sight in quickly, then fire. Keep it up. It's too late to conserve our ammunition," he told them. "We must stop them in the courtyard."

Following the brief mortar barrage, the SS again assaulted the courtyard, but their numbers were fewer. The defenders at the window met them with intense fire as everyone expended their ammo in one great volley. Maria unloaded an entire magazine from her pistol, expressing her rage lethally at the Germans charging her position.

Unable to penetrate the withering fire from the windows, Speers' attempt at a breakthrough to get inside the building failed miserably. The defenders again forced the attackers to pull back to the cover of the stone debris in the gateway. Two fell, struck by pistol bullets.

Jack was relieved but knew ammo was almost gone. How many more assaults can we withstand? he wondered. The first pangs of defeat ground at his insides.

The time to use the grenades is now, he immediately decided. "Get ready to open the door, Sarge. You and you… " He pointed at two GIs. "When he does, toss the grenades. Your best throwing arms. When they return, you and you go with the American grenades," he said, pointing to an Austrian and an American. He distributed a grenade to each man. "Do so, on my command."

The four men understood what he expected of them. They quietly nodded.

Jack turned to the remainder of American and Wehrmacht soldiers standing around him. "Fix bayonets!" he ordered. "If all else fails, we will charge into the garden to force them back across the bridge."

Sergeant Krouse translated for the Austrians.

Both Americans and Austrians looked at each other. First, the Americans and then the Austrians pulled their bayonets and fixed them to their weapons—M-1s and Mausers. The action was one every soldier understood and trained for, but never wanted to face. It was the finale in too many battles.

The soldiers gathered behind Lee, kneeling, prepared to run forward through the door and into the courtyard at the oncoming enemy, if ordered.

Reynaud and Maria stood behind him listening. "When all is lost," Maria said. "I will go with the soldiers. My husband is dead. I have nothing to live for." She inserted her last magazine, prepared for the end.

Reynaud looked at her. He wanted to hold her in his arms to soothe her but knew he must not. It was not the time.

"Maria, no. We will find a way out of this," Kurt said from behind her. He had just arrived from upstairs. He was the last person to vacate the ramparts high above them.

She turned to him. "I will never allow them to touch me again," she replied. "So it is better this way, I think."

"Josef would never understand," Kurt said. "You must never give up hope. The attack is weakening. I can see it. Please Maria. They are also low on ammo."

"Is everyone ready?" Jack asked Reynaud.

"I owe everyone so I will lead the charge," Kurt said, pushing Maria aside. "Everyone is gathered here in this hall," Reynaud said. He looked at the guns pointed out the window, but he knew everyone was out of ammo. "This is it, isn't it, Captain? I think everyone must charge them."

"This is it," Lee replied, looking around at the faces. He saw fear in those faces, yet there was also a strong determination to survive. Somehow, somehow… Deep inside himself, he prayed for a miracle.

Joaquin Speers knew defeat on the battlefield. He had personally witnessed it in Russia, and across Central Europe. But his men had always fought bravely and honorably. They always had the option of a tactical and strategic retreat. Now was different. They were trapped. Nowhere could they escape to find sanctuary. With tank fire coming from the road to Worgl growing closer, he knew all was lost.

CHAPTER 21

Major Speers, his wounded shoulder bandaged, braced himself against the rear of a Tiger. He caught only partial views of the action, but he understood what was happening. He watched his soldiers pinned down in the arch, and immediately grasped the gravity of their situation. "Too slow. They will be here soon," he hissed at the lieutenant, pointing down the road. "We should be in the castle by now. It has been more than an hour since we attacked."

"The defenders have fought well, sir," the young man replied. "But reports indicate they are almost out of ammunition and must surrender soon."

"Ha! Lieutenant, you do not understand," Speers said to admonish him. "They have nothing to lose. They will fight to the end. We should have offered reasonable conditions for surrender. I have been foolish."

"A flag of truce, sir?"

Speers smiled. "So foolish you are. They know we are SS and none would trust such a ploy."

They heard explosions and distant tank fire growing louder and closer. The sounds came from the direction of Worgl.

Speers scanned the immediate area closely. "We are in trouble." He looked up at the sky. Tank rounds begin to hit the area near the open field. An American P51 flew over and then two more suddenly appeared to the west. They flew low over the treetops. "Get down. They will return with their guns firing."

From the southeast, the planes banked to strafe his troops. They wore the markings of the American army.

"We are unprepared for an air attack," Speers said, already giving in to the futility of their last great battle.

The lieutenant, watching events unfold on the field of battle, saw men drop their weapons and run back into the forest. Then he, too, knew it was over.

Speers looked through his binoculars at the destroyed arch and his men moving into the courtyard supported by machine guns. His remaining tanks were still operational. They were very close to victory, yet…

He took the radiophone from the lieutenant's hand. Now a meaningless victory, he knew, but the attack on Schloss Itter had always been a foolish last effort toward a hollow triumph. He knew that, too. *Not for the Third Reich, but my own ego.*

Speers tried in vain to contact his infantry around Worgl to learn what was happening.

Artillery rounds screamed in, hitting the open field in front of the castle with much greater frequency. He heard the rumble of tanks coming up the road from Worgl.

One of his infantry commanders approached him from the field. His uniform was in disarray. Fear and defeat etched his features as he stood in front of Speers.

"Captain?" Speers said, dropping the phone to speak with him.

"Sir, the Americans have broken through at Worgl. Our men there are in full retreat, most running off into the forest. The Americans chase them and are very close."

"What are you suggesting," Speers asked but knew the answer.

"We have no choice but surrender. We must do it now. To continue fighting is futile, Herr Major."

"Pull your men back from the castle and form a line across the road to slow their advance," Speers ordered.

"Sir?" the captain seemed confused.

"You heard me. Re-form across the road," he said. "Then we will show them a white flag. We will try to parley with them." He knew the futility of that, but his options were gone.

"It's too late. My men are abandoning their positions. I saw NCOs run from the fighting. They all fled into the forest."

Speers would hear none of it. "Do as I have ordered, Captain." He picked the phone up again.

"We are retreating, sir?" the young lieutenant sounded almost gleeful.

Speers' phone went dead. He lost contact with his commander in Worgl. Angry and frustrated, Speers threw the receiver to the ground.

The captain turned and left without another word. "Sir, what do we do now?" his young aide asked. "Where is the staff car?" Speers asked.

"Back there," he replied. "Hidden in the trees."

"Get it, damn it," Speers ordered. He left the safety of the tank's rear to walk closer to the field for a better look. The fighting around the arch was diminished, both sides now growing low on ammo. He felt for his Luger and strapped on his helmet. "An Officer of the Waffen SS must never surrender and be disgraced," he said only to himself, and returned to the safety of the Tiger to await the lieutenant.

The lieutenant, driving the staff car, pulled up beside him. Sporadic gunfire continued around them. "Major, we must go now. All is lost."

Joaquin Speers looked long and hard at the young man who he had always suspected of being a coward. "Are you ready to die for Germany and the Third Reich, my young lieutenant?" he asked.

"We must save ourselves sir," the lieutenant argued. "Get in quickly. Surrender is always a possibility but not for us," his aide said, urgency in his voice, mostly from fear for his own life.

The engine revved.

"Get out of my sight," Speers said. "Go to wherever, Switzerland maybe. You are not man enough to die as Waffen SS."

Without speaking, the young man put the car in gear and drove off down the road.

Speers watched him disappear into the trees, lost in the shadows of the deep forest. He then turned and walked from behind the Tiger, exposing himself to the open field. He prepared to stand and die beside his men, believing wholeheartedly that was what officers in the Waffen SS must do. Speers knew well Adolf Hitler's pronouncement to fight to the end.

Determined, pistol drawn, he passed the tanks to join his men in front of the gate. Looking one last time down the road, he saw his soldiers in their camo uniforms coming from Worgl, many running without weapons. They were fleeing, not retreating.

The few remaining men around the arch besieging the castle also saw their retreating comrades. Morale quickly disappeared. The attack faded, with more men dropping their weapons to escape into the woods.

"Fight! I order you to fight," Speers yelled. "We are SS. We are the best." But his orders did not persuade his troops. They ignored him.

Everyone including Major Speers saw the first of the Shermans moving up the road. The Germans' partially formed line across the road crumbled quickly. The American tanks entered the clearing. American infantry arrived behind them. They began to encircle Speers and his men. The last of his infantry threw up their arms to surrender. Tank crews raised their arms high in the air standing on top of the Tigers.

The American tanks moved rapidly across the open field to complete their encirclement of Speers and his battalion. Sensing a quick victory, the GIs triumphantly unfurled their colors to the defeated Germans, like victorious roosters in a cockfight.

Joaquin Speers knew immediately how the battle would end. I will never surrender, he decided, watching the scene behind him unfold. "For the Fatherland," he yelled and ran through the shattered old gate into the courtyard. He fired his pistol at the stone wall.

A defender rushed out the door to heave a grenade just as Speers crossed the open area. After tossing it, the American dove for cover, and Major Speers absorbed the full impact of the blast. He fell to the gravel dead only meters from where Major Josef Gangl fell. They lay in the rubble now disturbed only by the slight wind blowing the last of the fog from the meadow.

For two soldiers, the war was finally over.

CHAPTER 22

All firing gradually ceased. An eerie silence suddenly descended on the courtyard. Jack heard the growl of Sherman engines rumbling through the field between the forest and the castle. The rest of the battalion had finally arrived. About time, he thought, wiping the stress from his brow. With their ammo gone, he knew they could not withstand another assault.

He walked out into the courtyard, followed by Maria and his soldiers. German soldiers stood numb, arms extended high to surrender to the Americans. He looked around at the dead and wounded from both sides entangled in the stone and wood debris and shook his head. He saw Major Gangl's body partially covered with stones and dust.

Knowing Maria searched for her husband's body, he turned to her. "Over there." He pointed. "He's there with the American he tried to save."

Maria ran to the spot where he pointed. She kneeled to wipe the dust from his face. "Oh Josef," she cried, touching him. "Please help me," she asked soldiers with them. "I must carry him into the hall. Please."

Two GIs nodded and walked over to assist her. They removed the larger stones and pieces of timber from his torso, and then lifted him—one had his shoulders and the other his boots. They carried him into the hall.

"Oh Josef, my love." Maria wept as they carried the body indoors and lay him on the floor with the other dead. Others, including the French POWs, continued to carry dead and wounded into the building.

Helping with the wounded, Jack looked over to see an officer among the enemy dead as they lay them out along the building wall. He bent down for a closer look. "An SS major and he died with his men. A waste when the war is so close to ending," he said, shook his head, and moved on.

"Hey Corporal, those two Nazis… I don't see them."

"No sir, I think they're inside."

"Get them out here. We need to retrieve the German dead and wounded from the field. That's a good job for them."

"Right away, Captain."

Jack returned indoors with his two sergeants. He saw that their many wounded—Austrians and Americans—were cared for. He looked over to the two rows of dead and saw Maria still with her husband. A strong woman, he thought. What will she do now? How will she survive alone in a devastated Europe? He removed the cigar from his mouth. Of all the young widows he had encountered in his bloody journey from the beaches of France, she affected him the most, and after less than 24 hours. She seemed so alone in a world she knew nothing of, but strong and determined, he decided. She will survive.

"Come on boys. We need to form up an honor detail for the KIAs," he said. "Corporal, get Sergeants Krouse and Glenn to assist you. I want a combined Wehrmacht and American honor detail." He pulled him aside. "We want to show the Frenchies how a real army honors its dead," he whispered.

The soldier looked at him but nodded. "Right away, sir." He left in search of Sergeant Glenn.

Jack removed his helmet and approached Maria. Paul Reynaud stood beside her, offering comfort. "My dear, an honorable and compassionate man," Jack said softly and compassionately. "An extraordinary soldier and adversary." His hand held hers. "We fought against each other across France, yet he is a terrible loss for everyone here."

Jack stood at attention. Six soldiers with the two sergeants joined him. "Maria, I would like to honor the dead of this battle, both Austrians and Americans who have fallen."

"Thank you, Captain," she replied softly.

"Very skilled and experienced soldier," Reynaud added. "A show of respect. I agree," he said, sounding very much the statesman.

Jack turned to the two NCOs and nodded. Both in English and in German, they formed up the men with their rifles—M-1s and Mausers. "Everyone gather around to pay our last respects to the men who so gallantly gave their lives for our survival," he said loudly so everyone in the hall could hear.

Everyone assembled, including GIs who had only minutes before arrived with the advance of his battalion.

Maria stood, drying her tears, with Reynaud still beside her.

"Present arms," Sergeant Glenn ordered with Sergeant Krouse quickly translating. All six soldiers presented arms.

"On behalf of the United States Army and all here, who fought to hold Castle Itter, I pay my respects to the men who gave their lives—heroes all. And to Major Josef Gangl, a tough adversary and a brave honorable comrade. We salute the brave men who lay before us." He saluted. Others behind him placed their right hand to their heart.

The ceremony concluded, everyone returned to jobs except Maria. She again knelt. She touched her husband's face one final time, thinking of their last night before he left to fight in the horrible war. Their wedding night, October 4, 1941…

Maria was alone with her husband, surrounded by the lush beauty of the estate's fields and woodlands. The night was late. They held hands walking through a fall garden, the colors and the smells, which they both enjoyed, shimmered in the moonlight.

She stopped abruptly, frowning as she looked over the uniform he wore—that of a Wehrmacht officer of the Third Reich. She touched it, feeling the heavy wool fabric.

"Josef, why must you go? Why not let Hitler and his minions fight. It is not our war as Austrians. Kurt is the Nazi, and we have given enough already with him fighting in Russia." She placed her head against his chest. "I won't let you go. You are mine, not Hitler's."

"I must stand beside my brother," he replied solemnly.

"Rolf worries. So many are wounded and dying there," she said. "Russia, like a vacuum, sucks in so many good men and spits out corpses."

He looked at her surprised by the analogy. "I fear it will get much worse. The Russians refuse to surrender even though they have lost millions of men already."

Josef smiled. They kissed long and passionately. "To leave you is the greatest sacrifice of all, my darling," he whispered.

"We can go to Paris like we talked about that summer which now seems so long ago. No, that's no good," she said. "The city now belongs to Hitler. New York then. We can afford to travel there. Free, we will be bohemians and lovers in New York City or go to Hollywood among the stars."

He again smiled, loving his wife's naiveté. "Darling, I'm afraid it's far too late for any of that. We Austrians are part of the Third Reich. The people have decided, and it is my duty to serve. For Austria as well as Germany."

"My husband, your duty is to me not Hitler."

"My duty is to you, but I also have a duty to Austria. Please try to understand that." He touched her face, felt her eyes on his soul. "No matter where I am, how far from here I must go, we will be together always. Always, do you understand?"

"Come, my husband. It is our wedding night." She took his hand, and they walked quickly back to their bedroom. There they made love, passionately but with a sense of urgency driven by fear and anxiety. They did not know when or if they would ever see each other again.

Maria thought of that moment and later when they lay together, with their lovemaking complete. She believed she could almost touch the stars and the moon. How hopeful yet fearful for our future we were. Then those bastards took everything from us. Her sorrow quickly turned to rage. She stood and walked toward the open door and pulled her pistol.

Reynaud watched her with growing concern. "Maria?"

She looked straight ahead into the courtyard. "I will kill the bastards who did this," she said, her grief quickly turning to anger.

Jack also noticed the quick change in her behavior. He heard her. "Wait! If we discover criminals among them, they will be tried and executed. That I promise."

Reynaud caught her as she entered the courtyard. "The battle is over, my dear," he said to caution her. He grabbed her shoulder. "See, they are surrendering. The war has finally ended for us, and we have won." But he knew the excitement and relief he felt were lost on her. She saw only the loss of her husband. He was saddened but he knew there was little he could do for her.

Maria stood in the rubble under the devastated arch, near where they found her Josef. She watched as American soldiers rounded up SS prisoners. With raised arms, they easily gave in to their fate.

Jack stood behind her.

She dropped her weapon and kneeled to the ground. "So much loss, so much killing. My Josef, my Josef," she said and began to weep.

Jack and Reynaud stood their distance and bowed their heads. From behind, Kurt ran to Maria.

"Maria, I'm so sorry. You have lost the love of your life, and I a brother."

She looked up at the SS captain. "This was your war, Kurt. Josef belonged to me, not to you and Hitler." Her tears continued to streak down her cheeks.

Kurt said nothing. He had no tears. He lost those somewhere on the Eastern Front long ago. He already recognized that now, as a captured soldier and as a member of the hated SS, he would be despised by the victors. He worried that he could face war crimes charges.

"Kurt, the locket. I'm wearing it," Maria said between sobs. She took it from around her neck and opened it. She showed him the small photos of two young men. "This is all I have to remember him. Everything is gone, but I will cherish this forever."

CHAPTER 23

Jack walked into the open field behind the destroyed tanks and slowly took in the battlefield where he had waged his final battle. He watched men from his battalion round up the remaining Germans who hid in the woods, and herd them into a containment area hastily set up in the open field. Disarmed, the captives were ordered to sit.

The SS soldiers were now defeated, their spirits crushed, yet they seemed more exhausted and hungry than fearful for their futures. Jack continued to watch them. I think I can understand, he thought. They are the Death Head Division no more.

The American tankers were out of their machines, smoking and joking. They too knew the war was over. Several were taking photos standing in front of the three Tigers. He smiled.

A jeep pulled up beside him. Jack saw the single passenger. He removed the cigar and spit. "Son of a bitch," he growled. He relit the cigar.

Major Kramer jumped from the jeep.

"Called it a little close didn't you, Major. Another fifteen minutes and they would have had us," Jack said. He saluted and they shook hands.

"They put up a strong resistance. That surprised me. I didn't think they had it in them," Kramer replied. "But you held them off like I knew you would. Good job, Captain. Damn good job."

"Yeah. We took a lot of casualties."

They stopped talking to watch the American flag rising above what was left of the front gate and arch. Cheers from inside the courtyard followed the raising.

"Tell me the bad news, Jack," he asked more somberly.

Jack removed the cigar and thought. "We lost four, and I think almost everyone else was wounded, several severe. The Austrians with us lost maybe five KIA, and most were wounded. Most of the wounds were shrapnel and flying debris. Luckily, only two among the POWs were wounded, no one killed."

"All things considered, that seems fairly light," Kramer replied. "You prepared a damn good defense, Captain, here and in that little town."

"Worgl?"

"Yeah, Worgl," Kramer repeated. "Very little damage there. Here?"

Jack smiled at the question. "All of it around the arch. Most of their rounds just bounced off the thick stone walls. They built them good back then."

Kramer and Jack turned to look at the castle. "Beautiful building. Belongs in the history books."

"I think it already is."

"Well, congratulations." Kramer shook his hand again. "You fought and won the last battle of this lousy war."

"Time to go home," Jack replied sullenly.

"Who's the young woman standing in the arch? One of the POWs?"

"She was a servant to them. Plucked out of Dachau before they hung her for treason."

Kramer looked harder at the woman. "Really? Fine looking woman. She's healthier than the others we liberated at the camps."

"Her husband commanded the Wehrmacht soldiers here. Both fought bravely against their own kind."

"Married then?" Kramer winked at Jack.

Jack took offense. "Widowed. Her husband died trying to save one of my boys." He pulled the cigar from his mouth to spit. He did not like the other man's condensation.

"Quite a story, Jack," he quickly replied, surprised by his captain's sensitivity about an enemy national. After all, they had seen hundreds during their sweep across Europe. "Again, good job." He turned to walk away.

"So God damn unnecessary," Jack called before Kramer was out of shouting range. "I wish you'd have sent someone else."

Kramer shrugged and continued walking.

Jack walked back to Maria and put his arm around her. Together they walked back across the courtyard and into the main hall.

"He died in combat saving another man's life. A real hero," Jack said again, trying to console her.

"A brave man," Maria said softly, head bowed. "Now I must move on alone back to the estate, or somewhere else. That I do not know. The Red Army is probably there drinking our wine and raping the local women. Isn't that what they do?"

"Horrible things happen in war, but remember, we are the survivors, and we must carry on. It's our responsibility to build a better life."

"I will do that. A world with no more wars." She looked hard into Jack's eyes. "It's the people, the civilians who suffered and lost so much. Like Bridget and me, and all the others. You will return to America and your family to resume your life but look around. What is left for us? Remember that, Captain."

"I will never forget," Jack Lee replied. He meant what he said.

CHAPTER 24

Maria watched silently as the French POWs except Paul Reynaud departed Schloss Itter, driven by American soldiers in requisitioned automobiles. "The Allies are taking them to Innsbruck to be honored by senior Allied Generals and others," a young Jeep driver told her.

Only hours earlier Captain Lee's men with members of the later-arriving casualty company buried Josef. Lee had asked what she wanted done with her husband's remains. "He must be buried here in the gardens with his men. Here, he gave his life to defend this castle and us, and here he shall lie," she told him. Following a brief ceremony, he and his men were laid to rest.

Maria went into the once-dangerous woods and picked wildflowers to decorate his grave. She placed them delicately on the mound of dirt. The remaining prisoners and solders did the same with the other graves.

"Someday," she told Paul, "I will order a great stone engraved with their names that befits their sacrifices. Yes, someday."

Paul Reynaud was the last to depart the castle grounds. He walked to where Maria stood. "My dear," he said. "You can come with me to France. I will make you comfortable until you find your way, or, if you desire, find you suitable employment in the French government." He loved her as a daughter or was it something more? Of that, he was not certain, but it no longer mattered.

Maria looked at the older man and smiled. "Thank you, Paul. You are very kind, but I am Austrian not French. I am all that's left of my family. Kurt is now a prisoner of war, and his fate is unknown. Such irony, I think."

"What will you do?"

"I must stay in Austria. It is my home. I will help to rebuild and create an Austria where everyone is free and equal. Yes, Equality, fraternity, liberty," she replied with a smile. "But thank you."

"I'm proud of you. A true hero to all of us who fight here," Reynaud replied. "I believe you will succeed." He turned to leave but felt compelled… perhaps for his own reasons, to say, "Please remember Maria. You will always have a home with me."

"Thank you, Paul," she replied. "I won't forget." "Nor will I," he replied.

"We have been through so much here during these months, given so much. Now I feel disconnected, alone and an alien in my own land," Maria confided. "I must be prepared for anything."

"You are strong. You will contribute to a new Austria. Of that I'm certain."

Appreciating his support, she smiled broadly, but still, deep inside she harbored doubts about returning to her only home. "I will never forget my Josef, but, yes, I must move on. Start a new life."

Later, when the French had departed, she sat alone with the other servants inside the great hall. American soldiers continued to arrive. They seemed busy performing those tasks that must be done following any battle since ancient time. They scurried through the hall, worked out in the courtyard and beyond the ruined gate, most dealing with the dead and wounded of both sides. She thought back to the early days before the war, to the beautiful estate she called home…

I loved the gardens with their beautiful flowers more than anything. To walk through them each morning and smell the scent of roses, lilacs, sunflowers, was the perfect way to start the day. The two-hundred-year-old house had ten bedrooms and a staff of six to keep it in operation. Paintings covered every wall, beautiful oils collected since the 18th Century. Most furnishings were as old as the house. I had my very own room and a servant to attend me. She was very nice and so loyal. She called herself Marnie and I will always remember her.

Rolf assigned me the job of supervising the household staff. I ensured the linens were changed, the floors and furniture dusted, but what I loved most was the great kitchen. Here, I watched the old cook, Margarete, bake bread and deserts. Oh, the smells.

The land that Rolf rented to local farmers was fertile but rocky. They had farmed it for hundreds of years. The major crop was potatoes. Tilled fields were dotted with stands of hardwood trees—mostly great oaks. Deep forests covered the lower elevations of the mountains that surrounded the estate.

As a girl growing up in the household, Rolf provided me with tutors. The only pupil, they taught me every subject, and they ensured that I learned, but I was always a good student. Rolf encouraged me to play the piano. Sadly, I was not musically inclined and much more comfortable outdoors playing with other children or around the beautiful horses he had stabled. Rolf took great pride in them. When Josef and Kurt were away at university, the groom, Johann, and I went on long rides through the shimmering meadows, and into the village. We always chose the best mares to ride.

Rolf, who adopted me as a very small child, was a wonderful man who loved children. His wife, Emma, died giving birth to Kurt. He adopted Josef when his oldest brother and his wife in Vienna died suddenly in an accident, leaving a child. Josef was seven. He raised all of us as his own children.

During my childhood, I spent many wonderful hours with local farmers and their families. Through Rolf, I knew many villagers including Jews. I felt his passion for equality among the Austrian people. I grew to believe as he did.

Wonderful memories, she thought. Can I find that peace again? She hoped and prayed, but deep down she knew nothing would be the same.

Although a wealthy landowner, and as many said, the last of the Austrian aristocracy, Rolf was a man of progressive ideas. Following World War I, he fought hard to establish a viable democracy on the rubble of the Hapsburg dynasty. He disapproved of Kurt's support for the Fascists and Germany's drive to annex Austria. When he joined the SS, Rolf threatened to disinherit him.

In politics, Rolf shared little with his son. Earlier, he had befriended and financially supported Johann Koplenig, the leader of the Austrian Communist Party.

Kurt, as a member of the Nazi Party, had terrible disagreements with his father over politics. Worst of all, the Jewish question, as Kurt referred to it, had to be settled once and for all time, according to Kurt. He believed Hitler's solution was too extreme, but he supported removing all Jews from the Fatherland. Kurt did not have Jewish friends.

Maria spent her remaining time at the castle preparing for the trip home. Paul had departed for Paris. Knowing she had to leave eventually, she began to organize the few possessions she had. Yes, I will keep the pistol, but I must locate better clothing and shoes especially, she thought, hunting through the castle.

"When the armistice is agreed and the guns stop firing, I will leave," she told Bridget, now alone with her.

"I will go with you," Bridget told her. "I have no home, no family but you."

Maria at first said nothing, but quickly realized this was still Austria with its strong antisemitism. She knew there would only be trouble for the young Bridget.

"No, you cannot," she finally told her. "It is still too dangerous for you even without Hitler and the Nazis. You have a great future to look forward to, but not in Europe, I'm afraid. You must go with the others… to Palestine, perhaps."

Bridget understood. They hugged and Bridget soon departed from Castle Itter, leaving Maria with the soldiers.

The war in Europe ended on May 7, 1945, with the complete German surrender at Rheims, France. After six years, the guns went silent.

Maria sat silently at Josef's grave, feeling relieved that after so much killing and destruction, the war was over. She now knew she must return to her home, but what then? She harbored many doubts about what awaited her.

"I must do this for Rolf and Josef," she finally declared to the few remaining at the castle. "I owe them that."

She gathered up her meager belongings. With the only money she had given to her by Paul, she planned to walk most of the distance to her village near Krems.

She knew she must make the journey with thousands of other Austrians displaced by the war.

Maria touched the temporary marker at her husband's grave, looked one last time at the great stone castle standing wounded in the early morning light and walked east.

"I will return one day," she vowed, tearful. "Now I must go home to face another enemy." She knew that, although the SS and Hitler were gone, she had no idea what she would face. With Austria in ruins, the Russians in the east and the Americans and British holding the western provinces, she had to be prepared for anything.

I must make it on my own, but she knew the life she faced would be difficult. I don't have Rolf's wealth now. I don't have any money except the Francs Paul gave me. The thought made her feel uneasy.

I have my memories of Josef, she thought, but even those I must bury deep along with my experiences at the hands of the Gestapo and of the horrible battle. She knew it was the only way to start a new life. Bury my past, she thought, deciding what she must do. Sadness gripped at her heart. Farewell my love.

"Yes, I must forget." Maria whispered encouragement as she looked down the long road through the forest she must walk. "I am young and healthy, with skills to survive. I can make it." Yet she knew life would not be easy.

CHAPTER 25

Maria walked into the forest heading east down the same road the Tigers had come only days earlier. She immediately saw the damage caused by the battle. Burnt out hulks of machines, trees broken and shredded by bombs and shells were everywhere. She walked by the decaying remains of soldiers and civilians on the pockmarked road, all testament to the fighting. The bodies had yet to be collected by grave details of either armies.

Americans in their trucks and jeeps passed her and other refugees made homeless by the fighting. Men, women, and children moving in both directions clogged the roads. Seeing despair written on their faces, she was reminded of the boxcar she rode to Dachau a few short months ago. Now they go home, she thought as she walked beside a young mother with two children. Like me.

Occasionally, a truck with large white stars on the front and doors stopped and offered rides. Everyone crowded against the rear to get a space among the soldiers, but Maria chose not and stood apart from the rest. Her pride would not allow a ride in the back of a truck, especially with young soldiers. She had more dignity, she decided on the first day, watching the soldiers pick only the young women to accompany them. Other American trucks stopped regularly to hand food to outstretched hands. They were friendly but cautious, dispensing food, individual by individual. That way they could watch who they fed.

"Any Nazis or Commies among you?" a young private asked to mostly the men. She understood that begging was for many the only way now to survive, but she would not. By the third day on the road, hunger began to gnaw at her insides.

After all that has happened to me, I will not beg the Americans for food, she swore. I am an Austrian Lady, she repeated to herself. Not a common beggar.

The young woman she walked beside finally took pity and offered her several tins of what the Americans at the castle called C-rations. "Take them," she offered. "I have plenty for now."

Maria took them. "How can I repay you?" she asked.

The young woman smiled. "We must help each other to survive."

They slept in the woods that night. The four of them huddled close together for both protection and warmth. The next day, they parted ways. Maria stayed on the road while the woman with her two children turned south.

Her feet began to blister as the shoes she had found at Itter deteriorated, then rotted off her feet. She discarded them to walk barefoot. When the blisters broke and festered, she was forced to stop. Luckily, she was near a small village. She saw American soldiers everywhere. Curious, she thought, limping closer for a better look.

On the outskirts were row after row of large green tents with soldiers who appeared to be assisting civilians. Maria limped closer for a better look. Her feet by now were bleeding.

A jeep passed close as she limped along. "Stop!" a soldier ordered the driver. When the vehicle halted, the man who she saw was an officer walked toward her. "Fraulein, you need to see a doctor. Come," he said and helped her to the waiting Jeep.

She did not like the American taking pity on her but said nothing. The pain in her feet and legs was too great.

They stopped in front of a tent with the large red cross. "I am a doctor," the man said. "We'll take care of those feet then find shoes for you."

She smiled. "Thank you, Lieutenant," she replied.

"You speak English. Good, good," he said smiling. "Perhaps, you can translate for me." He pointed at a line of civilians. They grudgingly watched while he treated Maria. "What is your name?"

"Maria," she said. "Maria Von Eickler." "Where do you go?" he asked.

"I go east to my small village near Krems." "I see. In the Soviet Zone."

"Yes."

"You are now only one mile from the Russian lines. They have a roadblock set up and they will want to see papers. Do you have any?"

"I do not. I come from a concentration camp. The Gestapo took everything from me."

The doctor looked hard at her, examining her body more closely. "That's terrible, yet you look good… healthy, I mean."

"Thank you. That is good, yes?"

He smiled. "Yes." He looked around. Seeing a young private, he waved him over.

"Yes sir," the young man said, standing in front of the doctor.

"Please take this young woman—Maria Von Eickler—to the house where my quarters are, and find a room for her," he said, and as an afterthought, "find her good shoes and suitable clothes. She has a long trip ahead of her."

"Yes, sir." The private took Maria by the arm and escorted her out of the tent, her bare feet heavily bandaged.

Maria and Private Yocum—she quickly learned his name—entered a small village also filled with Americans. "Here is where Lieutenant Bascom is staying. Follow me."

Maria in her new boots followed him into the house. They were a little too big, but still better than walking barefooted across Austria.

"You are to find a room for this woman," Private Yocum told an elderly woman standing in the doorway.

The woman first stared at Yocum, then looked to Maria. She scowled, "The price is the same," she said in halting English. "Who will pay?"

"The Lieutenant."

The woman nodded. "Come with me," she ordered Maria. They went up a flight of stairs to a small room. Maria thought it was a closet. "You will stay here, Fraulein. A meal tonight at eight, after the American soldiers have eaten. What is your name?"

"Maria Von Eickler," she replied. "My family lives near Krems and I'm returning there."

"Ha! An aristocrat," the old woman said with a laugh.

"Why do you laugh?" Maria asked, perplexed and insulted by her treatment at the hands of this old peasant woman.

"With the Russians there, you will be an aristocrat no longer," she replied. "And here, you are just another refugee like all the others who pass through."

Maria said nothing.

That night she saw the doctor again. They spoke well into the night. Maria had first worried that the doctor would want something in return, but she soon realized he wanted nothing more than good company.

When she awoke the next morning, she packed her meager belongings and prepared to cross the checkpoint into Soviet-held Austria. The Russians, she found, were far more difficult to deal with, and very suspicious. She had to be interviewed by an intelligence officer before crossing. When she explained to him where she had been and why she had no documents, he seemed to understand. That kept her out of a detention camp but got her no further with her travels. She spent most of a day struggling with bureaucratic red tape, just to get papers to travel.

Finally, Maria decided she must lie, explaining she was a farmer's wife and had to return to plant a new crop. That got her a pass. With the Russian NKVD internal security everywhere in eastern Austria, she decided to tell the military authorities that she was a close friend of Johann Koplenig, who returned to Vienna from exile as head of the KPO, Communist Party. That got her an ID and passage through to the Estate.

I must visit him in Vienna, she thought. As a friend of Rolf's, he may be very helpful to us as we rebuild the estate. Although a Communist, the bond between Koplenig and Rolf had been strong, and she knew he had good contacts with the Red Army.

The trip had been arduous and sad for Maria. She saw that the Austrian countryside was in complete disarray. She had to stop and hide several times along the road while different factions fought for control. Nazis, she saw, continued to hold power in smaller villages. Everywhere there was not enough food. The fields lay fallow, the annual seasonal routine disrupted by the fighting nearby. The further east she traveled the more Russian soldiers she saw along the road and in many villages. Having heard many rumors of out-of-control Russians, she was fearful, and was careful to mix in with other refugees.

When Maria arrived at the estate, she found it in complete disarray. The buildings had been ransacked, paintings stolen, furniture destroyed, and servants gone, but the old mansion still stood. Weeds had overtaken the beautiful garden and the fields lay fallow. The beautiful horses were gone, which saddened her more than anything did. She located Rolf's grave in the family cemetery and said a prayer for him.

Maria walked slowly around the ancient grounds. Easily as old as Schloss Itter, she decided. She examined the buildings and the fields, finally finishing her tour on the front steps to the great mansion. How she loved it, and as a child, she had learned where every corner and hidden space was located. She stood in front looking up at the majestic brick and stone building. Windows were broken out. The lawns were overgrown. I guess I have much work to do, she thought, walking up the steps and entering through the partially open front doors.

The first rooms she saw shocked her. They were stripped bare of furniture. Rugs torn from the floors. Old paintings, some several hundred years old, were gone. She saw the outlines on the walls where they had hung for centuries. In the bedrooms, pieces of furniture were spared from the looting. The hand-carved bed frames were missing, but end tables and wardrobes still stood. The cooking area, very large to support the household, was covered in dirt, the great stove turned on its side.

Maria began immediately to put things in order. She was able to meet with farmers who had tilled the family lands for centuries, and together they made plans for the planting of crops. Seeds were difficult to come by, but she managed to persuade local officials appointed by the Red Army to supply them, usually from confiscated farms. Everyone seemed to recognize that feeding the people was a top priority.

In August, Maria became ill and confined to bed. She learned that she was pregnant and was both elated and frightened. Without a husband, she knew it would be difficult in such an environment to raise a child. She prayed that Kurt would soon return to help. That did not happen in 1945, so she alone restored the house. Still under-furnished, she hired neighbors to do the repairs. She borrowed money, mortgaging next seasons' crop. Working closely with tenant farmers, she was able to plant some of the fields and get a crop in '45. The local farmers grew to respect her for her hard work and keen insight while working beside them. She learned quickly how to manage the lands and her life.

In December, she raised enough money to purchase a colt from a neighbor she had known since before the war. She spent hours in a reconstructed stable grooming and training it. She called the very young stallion Jack. Jack was a luxury during hard times, she knew, but the youngster gave Maria great joy and reminded her of better days.

On January 15 of the New Year, a son was born. Maria named him Josef after his father. He would become her life, the only legacy she had of her husband. She resolved to give him all the advantages her husband had received as a child and young man—the best education and social contacts. She was determined to devote the next twenty years to baby Josef.

Not until late in 1946 did Kurt finally return to the estate. Held in a prison camp operated by the western allies and not the Soviets, the Americans and British closely scrutinized his record for war crimes, but he was finally released, and allowed to return home.

Maria saw immediately that he was not the same man she had known at Schloss Itter and certainly not the young man she had grown up with as a brother. Cold to her, angry, and indifferent to the needs of the estate, he spent his time sleeping and walking in the high forests. He drank considerably and was prone to violent outbursts, often taking his anger out on her and the farm workers.

He took no interest in her or her child and refused to participate in managing the estate. "My father's business," he told her. "I was never a part of it. I think we became enemies after the war began."

"But you must help," she scolded him. "I have a child by your brother."

Kurt seemed indifferent to her concerns. "I once offered you an opportunity to be with me, but you refused," he told her once when very drunk. "Now it does not matter."

After, they rarely spoke. Maria ran the estate and ignored him. She decided it was best. She feared he might lose complete control of his temper and harm her son. He contributed nothing to the management of the estate.

Meanwhile, the economic situation in Austria grew from bad to worse. Industry yet lay in ruins with the largest industrial center—Vienna—damaged badly in the last days of the war. The severe winter of 1946-47 and a cold dry summer drastically reduced the potato harvest. Food riots erupted in Vienna. Maria had sufficient surplus to feed the local peasants and the townspeople, but nothing was available to take to market.

Later in '47, Kurt announced that he was selling the estate and going to America. Within weeks of his announcement, he found a buyer. He gathered his things, and was soon gone, leaving Maria and Josef homeless. The little money he provided her was barely enough for her and her son to survive on. They had no choice but to move to Vienna. She was determined to find work, anything, to support young Josef and herself. With great sadness, she returned Jack to his original owner, but she vowed to return one day to claim him.

After the war, Vienna was a divided city much like Berlin. The victorious allies—Russia, France, Great Britain, United States—occupied it, each with their own sectors of occupation, even though the city was deep in the Soviet zone. The Republic of Austria was declared in April 1945 and a provisional government formed. Parliamentary elections were held in November; where the Social Democrats, Conservatives, and Communists would govern, but the victorious Allied Forces, would in reality, rule the country until 1955.

In addition to the best farmland, Austria's industry was concentrated around Vienna, and was heavily bombed by the Russians during the final month of the war.

At the end of the war, the Russians, who took Vienna in April 1945, dismantled much of the country's industry and transported entire operations—machinery and all—back to Russia. With its fields in ruins and its industries gone, the Austrian people were left destitute and without work.

Several years after the war, the United States offered Austria the opportunity to participate in the Marshall Plan. The government accepted, and with low-cost loans and hard work, Austria began to rebuild.

In Vienna, Maria approached Koplenig and begged for a job in the mostly Soviet-run industries. He took her and her young son in, and ensured she have a good job in the trades.

Soon she was trained and working, helping rebuild the severely war-damaged city. In 1948, the Work Council, dominated by the KPO, elected Maria to full membership, thanks to the influence of Koplenig. She rose rapidly in both the Communist Party and in the workers' movement in the Soviet occupied zone. The Red Army encouraged her growing power but was careful not to interfere in local workers' politics.

Maria took a lover that same year. Willy was a member of the same trade union as she. He had spent the war years as a worker, managing to avoid both the draft and the resistance. Koplenig approved and together they took a very small flat near their work.

She decided she needed a man, mostly to help raise her son, but like Kurt, Willy offered little assistance. He came from a bourgeoisie Vienna family that, through their connections and money, avoided many of the hardships of the war that others had suffered. Lacking a sense of patriotism, Willy's family, using their influence and connections with local politicians, managed to help him dodge the draft.

Willy was a handsome man several years younger than Maria. He held no strong political opinions, which kept him out of trouble both during the war and under Russian rule. He had experienced little of the war, other than food deprivations and the bloody fighting around Vienna in its last months that everyone had to endure. He had little understanding for what Maria had suffered in the war, and she soon gave up trying to explain. He seemed insensitive to her continued struggle with her demons.

"Willy," she said often. "Austria must be rebuilt, replaced by a new order based on the voice of the people. We must contribute." Maria believed in democracy and was determined to remake the country in the image of America. She remembered Captain Lee and his GIs, whose attitudes toward hierarchy and authority both fascinated and confused her, but she had found them refreshing.

Willy had little interest in change, but his primary preoccupation was making money. He planned and schemed to put enough money aside to start a business. "I will be my own boss, Maria," he told her. "A mechanic with my own shop. That is the future of Austria, and when the Russians leave, I will do it."

Her idealism amused Willy. "Now, the Red Army controls our lives so get over it," he told her. "It's a new world much like the old. We must make our opportunities where we find them and hell with everyone else. That's how I survived the war. Believe only in yourself, woman," he hissed at her.

Maria found his attitude unacceptable. Often, they debated their different views well into the night. "Someday, I will go to the American sector where they have freedom," she often told him. That declaration would change their discussions from that between two lovers to one of politics.

"But you're a Communist," he replied in a recent discussion. "They would never allow you in."

"I am a Communist now because I must be," she replied. "Here we have nothing, and I must work for change. The Party offers a message of hope, hope for a better future. The Russians will help us. They will help workers in our struggle with the bosses. That is the only way for a better life for Josef."

Her life at Castle Itter had taught her many things, and one of them was to adapt quickly when opportunity presented itself.

Maria's days with Willy were generally pleasant by her own admission years later. Willy was not harsh with Josef. "At least, he's helpful," she told her coworkers. "He's just not very brave, always refusing to take risks." Maria quickly realized she could never love him as she did Josef. She was the first to admit that sex was good, but she decided early in their relationship she would never marry him… or anyone else. *I've had one true love*, and she believed that had to be enough.

CHAPTER 26

The troubles began in Vienna, and quickly spread across the country. The various wage-price agreements succeeded in raising prices to help producers, but workers' wages were stagnant. The food situation grew more acute by early 1950. Farmers demanded higher prices to bring their commodities to market, but city workers could not even afford the basics. Barely surviving on their paychecks, the workers demanded a 15 percent across-the-board wage increase and food prices be frozen.

Maria grew worried. Would she be able to buy milk for Josef? "We must do something," she said to members of her workers' council. When she told Willy of her concerns, he shrugged. "We survived the war," he said. "We will survive this. They will take care of us."

Maria glared at him. "They?" she said. "They don't care about us as long as we work hard for them. We must talk, and make our demands known. Yes, threaten them."

Willy looked at her, aghast.

Within days, the workers' unions led by the Communists and socialists negotiated with the bosses through the first nine months of the year. Maria insisted on taking part in the negotiations.

Tension often colored the talks with both sides threatening to walk out. Finally, by September the talks collapsed. Huge strikes loomed as the workers became much better organized. The police mobilized. Both sides turned to the Soviets, but they refused to intervene.

The first strike began on September 26, 1950, in all zones of occupation in eastern and western Austria. The Workers Council hotly debated the next step forward. The Austrian government, too weak to react effectively, was immediately thrown into crisis.

"Strike now!" most workers in Maria's group demanded, but others fought for caution and a resumption of talks. Willy urged them to continue talking with industry representatives to avoid a walkout, but Maria, knowing industry was unwilling to make any concessions, decided with most members of the council that continued talks were a waste of time. "They are no different than the SS," she told Willy with growing anger.

"We don't have enough money to buy food and pay our rent. We must confront them now!" she said to Willy. "It is the only way we can survive here, don't you see?" Maria expressed her view as strongly at council meetings. Debate on that September day went into the late-night hours. Finally, the leadership gave into demands to take a vote, knowing how it would end. Several members argued for a cool down period. They scheduled a vote for early the next day.

Maria, like everyone on the council, also knew what the outcome would be. She had worked tirelessly to bring it about, despite Willy's misgivings.

The world watched. The Western allies saw a country moving dangerously to the Left and completely into the Soviet orbit. But for Maria and the others, it was simply a matter of survival. Higher wages and better working conditions were a right. Most felt they had no choice but to act and quickly.

She moved Josef to Koplenig for safety. "If something happens to me," she told the old man. "Care for him." He agreed.

"Strike!" The workers decided with limited dissent on the first round of voting.

The Socialists supported the Communists and Maria with the others pouring into the streets. By the end of that day, 120,000 workers were striking. The streets of Vienna were a sea of people. Maria, with many from the council, immediately marched on the rail station. Her group, now more than 9,000 strong, succeeded in capturing three stations by midday.

Maria marched proudly through the streets of the city with thousands of her comrades. The marchers passed huge mounds of rubble remaining from the war. Some held banners high above their heads; others carried bricks and stones, prepared to do battle. All were determined to change a world that had become one of toil and hunger for them. The war had ended five years earlier, but they saw few improvements in their lives. The bombing and the fighting had long ago ceased, but the hunger remained.

She remembered the last time she marched with others. In single file, three deep, they walked through the streets to the awaiting railcars, the SS ready to transport them to the concentration camps. It suddenly occurred to her that her enemies never really changed—only their uniforms. She vowed never to allow that to happen again.

She fought a sudden sadness as she walked through the streets with Willy at her side. *Five years and still I must struggle merely to survive.* Willy, after much persuading by Maria, had surrendered to the cause, but only half-heartedly.

That night in their halls and in the streets outside, her membership debated their next move. Many, Maria included, demanded they march on the government. "Now is the time," she said, "before they can organize against us."

Police and paramilitary units mobilized to stop them. The workers, still led by the Communists, prepared for a fight. Maria worried about Josef, but she knew she must continue. She marched as if she were again fighting the Nazis in Castle Itter, seeing her current adversaries as no different from the old ones. *Then the Nazis and now it's the factory owners and their government cronies,* she thought. Maria was quickly learning that the struggle for survival and basic human rights never changes… or ends.

"We must seize Stadkau Station and block the railroad," she exclaimed at the late-night Workers' Council meeting. Seeing wavering in her ranks, Maria spoke passionately, determined to mobilize the other workers in the council. "We must continue the fight. Move on the post offices. We must cut off all communication with the outside world. Only then can we be victorious and force them to concede. The Red Army will not stop us!" she argued to the council. "The workers are being ripped-off," she continued. "Long live the workers!" She raised her arm high in the air. All members followed with their fists raised high. "Free the workers!" they repeated in unison later that night as they marched through the streets 15,000 strong to continue their protest. "Higher wages for everyone," they chanted.

Now we are different from when we were marched blindly into boxcars, she thought proudly. "We will win!" she shouted.

The police, having mobilized from across the Soviet sector, were ready for them. The two groups clashed in the streets of Vienna before the government buildings. Maria's workers fought with clubs and rocks against the much better-armed police force. Dozens of casualties on both sides was the result, as they fought to a stalemate with neither side giving in.

The workers' leadership called upon the Soviets to intervene to protect them. The USSR's primary representative in their sector was the Red Army. Soldiers hit the streets to try to keep order, but following requests that traveled all the way to Moscow, the Red Army declined to support the workers. Feelings of betrayal swept through the men and women gathered in the streets engaged in combat with Vienna's police.

"The cowards. We don't need the Russians," she shouted to the others to embolden them.

Maria, in the vanguard of her group, marched through the ranks offering support as they battled, engaging police herself when confronted. Their strike force, composed mostly of workers from the oil fields nearby, finally broke through the police cordon surrounding the government buildings. Hundreds of workers surged through the breach led by the Workers Council members.

Empowered by their success, the workers marched into the national governmental office (OGB) headquarters, and within hours, had taken control of many of the offices. They immediately surrounded officials. Maria and other ranking members of her council forced their way through the angry group determined to negotiate with political leaders trapped in the building.

"We demand that you raise wages," she ordered the highest-ranking officials they could find. "The agreement negotiated among the Powers is unacceptable to us. No one is speaking for the workers so we must," she said.

"Sign this. I demand that you agree to our demands." She shoved the hastily drawn up document in their faces.

The senior officials under duress, without reading it, agreed to each of their demands. "Ja, ja, I will sign the decree," one promised her.

The workers present cheered as each official, fearing for his life, placed his signature on the document. Maria was not so naive as to think the agreement would hold tomorrow but standing in that office with her army beside her, she felt victorious.

Fighting between her comrades and the police outside the doors grew louder and much more threatening as police reinforcements arrived on the scene. But Maria was determined to get the signed document. She would hold it up for the world to see.

Suddenly, the great doors to the old government building collapsed and the police rushed in, swinging batons. The strikers were no match for additional and better-armed police. They were quickly overwhelmed. Rapidly forced back across the large room, they yelled obscenities and demands at the police, but they did not run. At first, they tried to form a line against the well-armed adversary, but as the forces against them grew in number, their line weakened.

"Give me the document," Maria ordered the magistrate, and she grabbed it from the table. She slid it into her vest close to her bosom. Despite the best efforts of those around her to keep the police at bay, they were soon surrounded. The worker's defense first eroded away and then collapsed, despite their leaders' pleas to hold steady. Maria's Communist comrades ran tirelessly across the collapsing perimeter yelling encouragement, but it was too late.

"Come Maria," Willy urged her. "We must flee this place or be beaten and thrown in jail." He grabbed her arm and pulled her along.

"Wait, I must stand beside the others," she replied, struggling against his grip. "We must stand together against them."

"Then you accomplish nothing," Willy told her. "Here we have lost, but we can regroup and return tomorrow."

Maria looked at him, disbelieving. "There is only today," she replied hotly. "Take this," she ordered him, and pulled the document from her vest to hand to him. "See that the newspapers get this. I want the world to see what is happening here."

The young man took the papers and fled through a rear door.

"Workers forever," she yelled and ran forward into the melee, joining with her brothers and sisters. The battle with the better-armed and organized police raged for two more hours. The workers, their line of resistance faltering, fought on, but bloodied and bruised, they finally were forced to surrender. Workers holding the rail stations held out longer, but the strikes in Vienna failed. Thousands surrendered to the police. Maria saw that they had no choice.

The police had them sit down on the cold tile floor with their hands in the air. When all the strikers were gathered and packed together in the plaza outside the government building, they marched them out of the city to hastily constructed large detention camps.

The lines of prisoners, many bandaged from injuries, marched three deep, the line stretching more than two city blocks. Heavily armed police flanked them on both sides, closely watching. In the distance across an open meadow, Maria saw rows of tents built temporarily to house them. She was relieved to see no smoke-stacks. The two experiences were very different, she knew, yet Dachau camps now haunted her even more. She forced her fears down.

Maria with the others was unbowed. They yelled obscenities at the police as they filed past. "Nazis," they hissed. "Gestapo."

"I'll remember you," Maria said to a guard standing near her. "Are you a killer, too?"

When she arrived with hundreds of others and entered through the hastily strung barbed wire to the tent city, she looked around in disbelief. Memories of Dachau came flooding back uncontrollably. What has changed in five years? Nothing. Must we fight another war for our freedoms? she thought, her anger exploding.

"We strike only for a living wage so that we can feed our families," she tried to explain to a police officer interviewing her later. "I was in Dachau with SS guards, and you are no better than they."

"Shut up," was the police officer's only response.

The next day spread across the front pages of European newspapers was the headline: "Government Agrees to Workers' Demands but is Forced to Surrender." When Maria heard she was relieved and proud of Willy. Now the world will know the plight of Austria's workers, she thought.

Following long days with little food, she was processed, and released along with the others. The Government and the occupiers met few of their demands and the plight of the workers continued.

Making matters worse, Maria had no job to which to return. Stopped at the gate to her factory, Maria's supervisor told her she was no longer needed. "We don't want troublemakers here," an older man in the personnel office said. "Go away."

"Another asked me what I had to offer if he found me employment," she told Willy angrily. "I will not sleep with a man for a job. Never," she hissed. "I was forced to think of the degenerate Nazi, Wimmer, as I stood there feeling his awful eyes on my body."

As the days passed, she canvassed the city, knocking on doors, but to no avail. Maria had been effectively blacklisted in Vienna. Her coworkers found themselves in similar positions. All vowed to leave the city for the West. Facing hunger, each understood they had no choice. Maria's determination to stay in Vienna faltered as she watched friends depart.

"I have worked and toiled to make a life for me and my child," she explained to Koplenig later in the evening of her firing. "I have fought Nazis, bosses, and capitalists these years, all of them just angry little men who want to keep me under their thumbs and in their beds. I refuse to allow that. Still, I have nothing." Too proud to weep, she stared at the floor with anger burning deep inside.

The older man listened quietly. The sadness in his eyes said it all. Finally, he spoke, "You must flee this world. Go west. There you will have more opportunities. And," he said, "I think you have no choice."

"How do I start over?"

"You are young and strong. You will find a way."

That week she packed and prepared Josef to travel. Where, Maria was not certain, but one thing was—out of the Soviet zone of occupation. After five years, she had had enough. She felt betrayed by the Russians with their failed promises and false ideals. No better than the Nazis. Their only interest was power and control, she decided.

The Americans are probably no different, she thought, but, at the very least, the West offered the hope of opportunity. Maybe there she and her son would have plenty to eat.

CHAPTER 27

Discouraged but not without hope, she returned to her small flat, grabbed her son, and her meager belongings. She fled Vienna, deciding to go first to her village near Krems. Five years of Russian hypocrisy and hunger were enough. She vowed never to return to Vienna. She left Willy behind to search for a better life. She had had enough of him, and she thought, he enough of me. His heroic and successful attempt to get the word out was not enough to stay with him, and she knew he would never leave Vienna.

In Krems, she wrote Jack and her friend Paul letters daily—to Paris and to America. While working in Vienna, she had made many friends who had fled the city for a better life in the West, and she knew wanted to stay in Austria outside the Soviet zone of occupation. Maria decided she would live in the American sector, much like her friends.

With the New Year, Maria began to worry that, with her meager savings dwindling, she had to leave Krems to find work. She knew she could not stay in the village much longer. Her only friends were poor farmers, having suffered under Soviet control as much as she had.

"I must leave for the West, but I will return to Schloss Itter to visit my husband's grave on my way," she told them. She packed up Josef and soon was on her way to the old castle. Mostly by old bus, the two made their way first to Worgl, and then by foot up the mountain to Itter.

They stood in the small meadow where so many had died. She stared at the great stonework still standing guard over the Tirol as it had done for centuries. Maria looked round the meadow slowly, trying to take everything in. It all seemed so serene. Six years ago, I saw only horror. Tanks and soldiers attacking, smoke and shrapnel flying. Places on the great granite walls were still pockmarked, some severely cracked, and even shattered, where the big guns hit it repeatedly.

Maria was surprised to see workers on scaffolds working on the old and damaged walls. They worked on the arched gate where the SS tanks killed her husband, much of it already restored. The workers heaped the stones on a pile nearby. Why? she asked herself. Will they build a museum, a monument to those who fought and died here? She could only hope.

She entered the courtyard where large chunks of stone were stacked. Ghosts everywhere, she thought as she walked by the spot where Josef had lain, killed by an explosion. Still, she could not stop. It hurt too much. Maria, silently with tears forming, tugged young Josef along to walk quickly to the main entrance to escape the pain.

Entering, she looked around surprised to see workers everywhere. What is happening? she wondered, surprised by all the activity. She stopped the first person she saw she thought was in charge. "What are you doing here?" she asked.

"This will be a hotel," the man replied.

"What!" she exclaimed. "No, it cannot be. A desecration."

At first, the man just stared at her, then shrugged and walked away. "Wait. Who's in charge here? Tell me. I must speak to him."

The man turned. "Walter Wolfstein. He's the young man dressed in a suit.

You will find him in the kitchen with his plans."

She entered the large room, now empty of cooking appliances. She watched other craftsmen from the large doorway as they sawed and hammered on the wood and stone. Dust filled the air. She would never forget serving the French as a slave and servant. Even without the great stove and many cupboards, the memories were still unavoidable.

"Mamma, who are they?" Josef said, pointing to a man standing on a high scaffold near the window.

Maria looked to where her son was pointing. She recognized that window immediately. She had fought the Nazis from that window.

A well-dressed man approached her. "May I help you, Fraulein?" he asked politely.

"Who are you?" she replied. "I'm looking for Herr Wolfstein." "I am he," he said and stuck out his hand.

Maria absently took it and shook but she was obviously distracted by the changes she saw.

He watched her silently.

"What is happening here? This, this cannot be... I protest." "I beg your pardon?" He was confused. "Who are you?"

"I am Maria Von Eickler and my husband was killed here fighting the SS," she said, having to force out each word. "He is buried on the grounds along with others."

Recognition flashed in his eyes, and he smiled. "I've heard of you, of the battle fought here. Come, please... Coffee?"

"I must take my son to his father's grave. May I or has it been moved... to make way for a swimming pool or something?" she asked sarcastically.

"Oh no, we would never do such a thing," he replied, with all seriousness. "Please, after, we will talk. I will explain everything."

Following their visit to the gravesite, where fresh flowers had been placed on each of the clearly marked headstones, Maria re-entered the castle through a back passage. Someone cares for them, she thought relieved.

She returned to speak with Mr. Wolfstein one last time. He was directing workers in the great hall. They spoke for several hours; Wolfstein explained that he was building a luxury hotel.

"Soon the old castle with its many memories preserved will be open to guests who are interested in knowing about Schloss Itter," he said. "I did not fight in the war. Too young, but I experienced its horror with the bombings and occupation. And the hunger," he said sadly. "My father served in the West and was captured by the Americans—luckily."

"This is a place with so much suffering, where my husband was killed protecting us against the Panzers. An important part of my life will never leave this great castle. Please understand. For me, the castle stands as a monument to my loss."

"I promise I will never destroy those memories for you."

That day, Maria and Josef returned to Worgl to continue their journey to Innsbruck and their friends. Her primary concern was still survival, and she had to bury those memories deep inside. She also knew she was powerless to prevent Herr Wolfstein's plans for a luxury hotel.

First, she decided she had to walk the streets of Worgl, talk to its residents. Does anyone remember?" she asked herself. In a shop near the bus station, she found an elderly shopkeeper. I must speak with her, she decided. She remembers. Maria approached the woman.

"Madame, have you lived here long?" she asked. "Do you remember when the war came to Worgl?"

The old woman looked at her, a long considerate look. "I remember," she replied.

Maria grew excited.

"First the freedom fighters came and hid in our homes. They hid from the Panzers who they said were coming. Then a few Wehrmacht soldiers and they fought each other, but not very long. They met and arranged a truce. 'No more fighting,' they agreed."

"Then," Maria asked, urgently wanting her to continue.

"Another soldier came and he talked with the soldiers, then they all leave. Ahh yes, we believed that was the end. But no, the Panzers come. We believed they would kill us, everyone. We hear lots of noise and shooting begins everywhere. It's the Americans with their tanks. Soon the Germans surrender. I guess they know, too, that soon the war ends. That day we were liberated. Oh, so happy. Everyone celebrates. We were saved."

Maria smiled. "And the castle up there?" she asked, pointing to Itter.

"Ahh, the castle." The old woman looked up at nothing. "Horrible. Up there no luck. The Panzers attack and many are killed. All morning we hear the explosions, then more Americans come with their tanks. The fighting soon ended, I think."

"Did you meet anyone who was there… that the SS held captive?"

"Everyone leaves… almost everyone. My Franz told me long ago that a young woman remained for maybe two days. He brought her food. But then she leaves, too."

Maria looked at her, eyes filling with tears.

The old woman smiled. "You are the lady in the castle."

CHAPTER 28

Shortly after arriving in Innsbruck, a letter arrived addressed to her. Maria looked at the postmark. Two months it had taken to get to her via Vienna. "Paul!" she said to Josef excited. "Paul, the great premier of France, has written me." But Maria was under no illusions. His secretary may have written the letter, or it is bad news, she thought hesitantly. She had not heard from him in almost six years. Anything could have happened in that period.

Maria, filled with anxiety, opened the letter.

My dearest Maria Von Eickler, hero of the Battle of Schloss Itter,

She smiled and continued to read:

I have thought of you often and I am saddened to hear of your struggles.

Maria read on, enjoying the wonderful letter, of him discussing the beauty of the French countryside, and on a much more somber note, of the political struggles convulsing the French Republic.

I want you to come to Paris and I will assist you in finding an opportunity. I know, whatever you attempt, you will succeed in accomplishing. I will never forget your bravery and leadership, but most importantly, our friendship.

Enclosed, Paul Reynaud included a rail ticket from Innsbruck to Paris and sufficient French Francs for her and her son to travel comfortably.

She wrote him back:

Paul, thank you for your great generosity. I will accept your offer but only for a short visit. I look forward to seeing you again, and I have dreamed of visiting Paris for many years. I, however, must continue my fight to build a good life for my son and me here in Austria. I know that will happen and I cannot give up until I am successful. See you soon.

Her life for more than ten years had been one of survival—first the war and the loss of her beloved husband, Dachau concentration camps, and later, economic struggle in post-war Vienna. She had had enough of the constant battle just to eat, and her son deserved better. She hoped life in Innsbruck would be better than life under Soviet control. *I must make my home here with my friends,* she decided, determined to stay.

She believed all she needed was an opportunity, and the Americans were pouring money into Austria as well as Germany. *I will work for them.* She marched from factory to factory to request work and at each, they told her to wait. "Come back tomorrow," they told her.

The days passed. She waited and hoped for an offer of employment. Frustrated, Maria decided to try the U.S. Army, which still operated several camps. At first, looking at her papers, they were cautious. Maria possessed a passport, but she lacked papers for travel outside the Soviet Zone of occupation.

"Why did you leave Vienna?" a personnel sergeant asked during an interview. "I am a refugee. I flee the Communists," she told him.

"We must check your story before we can hire you. The Russians are dangerous, and we can't allow spies to enter our zone," he said. "We will notify you when you're cleared."

Just like during the war, she thought, but said nothing. She left quietly, wondering if she should have any hope for employment. *Another war is coming, and the people will suffer,* she thought sadly on the tram back to her apartment. *They play us like pawns in a great game of chess.*

Feeling she had done all she could to find work, Maria decided to take Paul up on his gracious offer. One week later, Paul greeted her at the Paris train station. He held a bouquet of flowers to present to her. He seemed surprised at seeing a six-year-old child with her. *She has not changed,* he thought, still admiring her beauty. Handing her the bouquet, they embraced.

"Paul, so long," Maria said, smelling the flowers. "Thank you. They are beautiful." He has aged, she thought, looking him over. Yes, much thinner and so frail.

"Yes, the years have passed," he replied. He looked at Josef and smiled. Maria could tell it was heartfelt.

"Oh, my Josef," she said. "Josef this is Paul, my old friend from the war years."

They shook hands and Paul smiled. "The father?" he asked, unable to contain his curiosity.

"Josef... my husband," Maria replied proudly.

"Such a handsome young man," he said. "I think he looks just like his father." Soon, Maria and Josef were enjoying the sights of the city, and Paul ensured they were treated first-class wherever they went. She felt reborn with renewed hope. His health prevented him from accompanying them, but he assured Maria his heart was with them.

At night, they spoke of their days at Castle Itter. She never told him of Herr Wolfstein and his hotel. That experience still troubled her, and she did not want to upset the old man.

Paul told her that he believed he had fallen in love with her during the battle. His admission surprised Maria. Not knowing how to respond, she looked down to avert his eyes.

"Please, don't be embarrassed," he said with a smile and touch of his hand. "We French are always in love with a beautiful woman, eh?" he said, as if it were a matter of French pride. "We try in that way to hold onto life... with its many pleasures." He continued to watch her, appreciating her company. And it was good to have a child running the grounds again.

She could only smile in return.

Later, Paul urged her to accept a position in France with him as an English, French, German translator, but she declined.

"I am Austrian and will remain so, but thank you," she told him delicately. "When I return, a position awaits me," she lied.

He seemed to understand. "France needs citizens like you."

"I must make it on my own. That is most important for me," she said, not wanting to hurt him.

He again smiled softly. "Yes, Austria needs its best and brightest. Our loss, Austria's gain."

She would never forget his smile.

Paul accepted her decision without argument, which surprised Maria. She had expected that he would insist, even suggesting a job. Curious, she thought, knowing how persuasive he could be.

Maria and Josef departed for Innsbruck a day after their discussion.

Maria returned to Innsbruck to find good news. The Americans were interested in her skills, and they told her they were considering her for a position. Soon, following a week of impatient waiting, she was working with the U.S. Army. She thrived, acting as interpreter, eventually for American command.

Several months after their visit to Paris, she received word that Paul had died of cancer. Maria had known the end was near. Paul's daughter informed her the day she departed. Yet the loss of her friend devastated her.

By the mid-fifties, Western Europe began to boom with American money fueling its revival. She found her opportunities and left the U.S. Army after several years to open her own business, quickly rising to become very successful and wealthy. She traveled frequently throughout Europe.

She made a single trip to the United States on business, but she was most interested in locating Captain Jack Lee from Texas. She failed to locate him but met many wonderful people whom she would never forget.

CHAPTER 29

Maria was determined that Josef receive the best education Europe or America offered. She immediately thought of Texas. When it was time, she packed the young man off to America to enroll at Texas Tech University. She based that decision mostly on her fond feelings for Texans rather than on any academic criteria. Soon the young man was an American student. He excelled in his first year.

By his sophomore year, he was spending time getting to know the new country with his American friends. He traveled extensively, visiting New York, California and a host of historical sites, but mostly, his interest lay with finding Jack Lee. His mother over the years had filled his head with many stories of the American tank commander. He was motivated to learn more, or better, to meet the man her mom made famous.

"Dear Mama," Josef wrote from his dorm room the spring of that year. "I've found him."

Upon reading her son's letter, Maria was so excited she dropped everything to reply. She had made several trips to the United States since Josef had begun attending Texas Tech University. Her searches for the tank commander always ended in failure. It was as if he had dropped off the earth... or died. Their American savior with his tanks left Austria by way of France and had returned to the States several months following the battle for Castle Itter. She learned that through her contacts in the U.S. Army.

Josef, thanks to his mother, was a very resourceful young man. He learned the Americans had national veterans' organizations with large memberships. He wrote the American Legion and the Veterans of Foreign Wars, two of the most well-known of them. He received a reply from the American Legion stating they had forwarded Josef's letter to the veteran. That was all they would do. Josef hoped for a reply. January of 1964, he received a letter in the mail. Seeing who it was from, he opened it excitedly and read: Josef, the letter began...

I remember your mother well, and pray she is in good health. I am surprised she has a son, and he is attending university here in the States. The writer spoke highly of his mother and went on to explain his dealings with Josef's father during that very brief but intense period. Jack told him his life had also been difficult since his discharge from the U.S. Army. He was the father of one son and a daughter. His wife was killed in an auto accident in 1951. He had had many jobs to support his family, but sadly, he said, none made it to the level of his job in the army. He provided Josef with an address.

Josef saw that he was currently living in Indianapolis, Indiana.

Maria learned to be careful when discussing with the past with war veterans. One never knows what ghosts are freed once Pandora's Box is opened. The loss of Paul had disturbed her greatly. She had lost a true friend when he passed. But she quickly decided to take the risk and bought an airplane ticket for Chicago. There she planned to meet her son and together they would travel to Indianapolis.

The drive from Chicago was quiet, both lost in their own thoughts. Finally, Josef spoke, "Mama, what will you say to him? If you don't recognize him? Remember it's been twenty years."

"Yes," she replied. "A long time. I've thought of him so often and searched everywhere. I want to talk about Castle Itter and our time together. The captain and I share that horrible experience. I need to know what he remembers."

Finding Jack Lee's home was not difficult. He lived in a small bungalow in a middle-class section of the city.

They walked to the door, Josef holding his mother's hand. Before they had a chance to knock, the door opened. Captain Jack Lee stood in the doorway. He beamed from ear to ear.

"Maria," he exclaimed. "Please… come in." They embraced awkwardly, each looking the other over. Both hoped they would find some attribute in the other they recognized from twenty years earlier.

Maria saw that the years had weighed heavily on Jack. He was much heavier and as they walked across the living room, she saw a slight limp. His hair was turning gray and thinning, but he still possessed the same good looks.

"Please sit." He said offering them both a chair. "Drinks?"

"No thank you, Jack." Maria spoke for both. They sat, then Jack sat in a chair across from them. The silence hung in the air at first, and then he pulled out a short cigar and lit up.

Seeing the cigar in his mouth, she laughed. The men both looked at her. "You still smoke, I see," she said. "I remember that so well."

"Since my wife died more than ever," he replied. "I hope the smoke doesn't offend you?"

Maria and Josef both nodded their heads. "I'm sorry to learn your wife has died," she said.

"Yes," he said. "Very tragic and me with two kids to raise." "Tell me about yourself. Your work."

Jack sighed and looked off, out the large window. "I sell insurance… sometimes."

Maria looked at him, not understanding. "Sometimes?"

"I've had problems—my wife's death, the war. My head gets scrambled, and I can't do nothing about it. I have bad dreams and when they are unbearable, I go to the VA—it's a hospital for veterans—and they give me meds. So I sleep a lot."

She was saddened to hear his story. "You were a good leader. I don't think we would have survived without you and your soldiers."

"I appreciate that. In many ways that is reassuring."

He smiled but a sad smile, she thought. "Your children?" she asked.

"They don't live close, not anymore. You see... I have this temper. I would get angry with them for no reason. It was bad so one day I sent them to live with their grandparents. I didn't want to hurt them." Jack spoke slowly and haltingly to force each word out, often hesitating. "I don't talk about the war much," he said. "It still hurts." He became tearful, choking up when he talked of his men.

"Do you keep in touch with them?"

"No, not so much anymore," he said with a shrug. "Tell me your story. I want to hear what happened to you after that day."

Maria spoke of her life—her problems after the war, the strikes in Vienna. "I was lucky, Jack. I moved to Innsbruck to find work. The Americans finally hired me. They urgently needed people who speak German, French, and English. I have been very successful in that work and today run my own business," she said with a smile. She spoke proudly of her accomplishments.

Jack listened quietly. "I knew you would survive and do well," he replied. "Now tell me. Why have you come all this way to visit me?"

Maria had to think about that. "I think... I think because that day in many ways shaped who I became. And Jack, I need to know more about my husband, Josef's father. Please tell me all that you remember of May 4 and 5, 1945. Can you talk about it?" She had met many combat veterans from different countries who could not. She saw that Jack was having difficulty.

"I want to, and I need to. The VA docs say to forget about the war, but I can't," Jack said, beginning slowly. Again, his voice was soft and hesitating. "I think about those men killed at the castle that day. I can't get it out of my mind. It hurts inside." He stopped, stared at the rug and then began again. "They died for no reason. The war was all but over. Their lives ended — so young and I was responsible. Every day I feel that guilt."

"No, it was war," Maria said compassionately. "You had no choice as a leader." She wanted to encourage him, but knew she had to be careful.

He again stared at his hands while forcing the words from his lips. "God will never forgive me. Your husband... sometimes I think I could have saved him. My fault. I'm so sorry." He held Maria's eyes with his own. "Every day I wrestle with that question."

Maria was saddened to hear him struggle. "No Jack, the SS killed him. He made his choices, and he fought like you to defend the castle."

Jack did not respond. Finally, he spoke more of the day he and his men entered the castle and met Josef and Maria. They were pleasant stories and he smiled.

Josef leaned closer when he spoke of his relationship with his father, not wanting to miss anything. Together, they laughed and cried.

"I think your husband and I could have been friends… but for the war," he whispered.

When they finished, as darkness descended on the Midwest, they hugged and said their good-byes. Each knew they would probably never see the other again, but they exchanged addresses and promised to write.

Maria departed feeling excited about learning more of that day, but she was disturbed at Jack's mental condition. That day at Itter, he was such a strong, take-charge leader, and she would always believe their survival was due to that leadership. This was not the same Jack Lee.

Twelve months later, a letter arrived from Indiana, USA. Maria looked at the return address and saw that it was from Jack's son. She opened it with grave misgivings, worried that something had happened to Jack. Her worse suspicions were confirmed. The short letter began:

Dear Mrs. Von Eickler, I have bad news. Two weeks ago, my father took his life.

Maria read on.

My father left a note. In it, he wrote a brief message that he wanted me to pass on to you. "Castle Itter still holds our deepest memories and our sorrows. We must confront them and protect them, Maria. You are much more capable to face them. I am not strong enough."

Protect those memories? Maria asked herself. I've been trying to bury them—the good and the bad—for 20 years. She thought long and hard over his message. Is it now time, she wondered? My son will soon graduate from college, and I'm prosperous enough. But where do I begin? Castle Itter. Yes, that's where I must go.

She had not been there since her visit in 1951. She considered what the castle would look like today. Did they turn it into a boutique hotel for American tourists?

The world had changed. Austria was now free of foreign powers, and times were good for its people. Yes, we've moved on, she thought proudly. But, has the world forgotten the war and its survivors? Have its heroes, men like Josef, Jack, and Kurt, been relegated to the dustbowl of history? Those questions began to haunt her.

No, I cannot allow that, she decided. "Those memories shaped my life. They are who I am," she wrote her son. "The war and its heroes must be remembered, learned from, and that requires more from us than merely visiting cemeteries. This is where my life leads me. That will be my legacy to you and your children." Josef understood.

He graduated from Texas Tech in 1967, and his proud mother was there. The young man returned to Austria as an engineer like his father. Josef accepted a job and a life in Vienna. He's close, Maria thought relieved.

The years passed. Her business was not so easy to step away from. Her son married and soon a grandchild was on the way, then another. She became the doting grandmother, marking time constantly traveling between her home in Innsbruck and her son's in Vienna. Yet, she never forgot her vow.

Finally, that day arrived. Never fearful of taking action, Maria decided without any doubts that it was time to uphold her promise to the past. Her grandchildren were growing up, Josef was successful in his profession, and she had sold her business. She was free to embark on a new adventure. In early June 1985, she packed her bags and departed for Castle Itter.

CHAPTER 30

May 5, 2000, Worgl, Austria

An old woman sat in a wheelchair near a fountain in the main square of the small village. Her face deeply lined and her hair gray, yet her beauty, faded from the years, still shone through. The street crossing the square was clearly marked "Strauss Gangl." The woman was speaking to mostly American tourists who now gathered around her after a tour of Castle Itter.

Maria dedicated the remainder of her life to preserving Castle Itter, with its memories. When first arriving, she carefully researched its rich seven hundred years of history, and she told its story to thousands of tourists each year. Mostly, she spoke of the horrible battle that had killed her husband and many others. She believed it important that everyone understand that Austrians, French, and Americans fought side by side against the might of Hitler's infamous SS. "The great battle of Schloss Itter," she called it.

She wanted everyone to understand why the castle and village of Worgl were so important. "For my children and their children," she said. "For me... I must reach out, not for the future—I am old and have none—but to the past. I want only to hold onto a small piece of its history, so that I will always have a memory of my husband that glows bright and warm in my heart."

"We stood together against the forces of evil," she told her audience. They listened quietly, enthralled by the old woman's storytelling.

She looked up at the street sign and smiled. *A memory I can even touch,* she thought.

"I have told you my story of Schloss Itter and of the brave knights who defended her," Maria said. "As you've seen, the castle still stands in all its majesty after 700 years." She concluded her story with a sad but hopeful smile. Her eyes sparkled with pride.

"Did you ever live in that castle?" a little girl asked, stepping forward from the group of mostly Americans who had clustered around the old woman.

Maria smiled at her. "Yes, my dear. I lived there for a short while. I was held there as a prisoner for two months, then the Panzers came. They attacked us and we fought Hitler and his minions on its high walls. The SS wanted to kill us all. We won the battle, but I lost the love of my life."

While Maria was speaking, a late model Mercedes pulled up behind the group, a well-dressed, middle-aged man and two younger men, quietly walked up to the group.

"Did you see the name on the street marker?" "Yes," the girl replied.

"The sign was named for my husband, Major Josef Gangl, who fought alongside the Americans to protect us. He was killed trying to save an American in the great battle against the SS." Maria reached to her bosom to touch the locket around her neck, her most precious possession.

The girl watched her. "What's that?" she asked curious.

Maria said nothing but removed the locket. She opened it for the girl to see. At that moment, Maria caught a glimpse of the man and two youths accompanying him. The three approached her to stand beside her and the little girl. They silently listened to the old woman as she showed the child the locket.

"Who are those boys?" the girl asked, touching the gold locket.

Maria pointed to each of the two boys. "He was my husband, Josef, and the other is Kurt, his brother."

"Do they live here, too?"

"Josef was killed here at Castle Itter, and Kurt went to America long ago. I never heard from him again."

The little girl looked sad.

The man reached down to touch Maria, placing his hand to her face. The youngest of the two men standing beside the wheelchair hugged her close.

"Gramma," he said, kissing Maria on the forehead.

"Josef, you've come for a visit. I'm so happy," Maria said, her hands close to her heart. "And you've brought my grandsons. What a wonderful surprise." The tourists watched. They felt good about the unexpected reunion.

"Mama," the well-dressed man replied. "It is always good to see you here with Papa."

The little girl smiled.

"You see," Maria said smiling softly at the girl. "We must hold onto our past with all its memories. Then we can find our way in the future. Schloss Itter is a monument to that war, but my stories are for the future. They are for you, child, for generations to come. I want you to understand that horrible war and the suffering it caused." She looked up at the other tourists and to her grandsons. "And for everyone… ," Maria said in a strong proud voice, "please do not forget us." Tears filled her eyes.

THE END

Other fine books available from Histria Fiction:

For these and many other great books visit

HistriaBooks.com